MW00961537

Keeping Captain

N. L. Sharp

Published by Prairieland Press
PO Box 2404
Fremont, NE 68026-2404
Printed in the U.S.A.

ISBN for Print Version: 978-0-9759829-8-3
Library of Congress Control Number: 2015959863

Prairieland Press™

For my sisters Charliss and Corliss,
who make barrel racing look a lot easier than it is.

Chapter 1
Practice at the Castle

Nebraska, 1967

Carly steered Captain in a tight circle around an imaginary barrel. Then leaning forward, her hands resting on either side of the big Quarter Horse's neck, she let him fly down their lane.

As she raced past the windbreak of pine trees that led from their farm to the Carsten Castle Estate, she grinned. Today was the first day of summer vacation and the first time she and Luke could officially call themselves sixth graders. She had been waiting for this day ever since kindergarten.

When Carly reached Luke's front gate, she slowed Captain to a trot. Mrs. Carsten was serving coffee to a couple on the veranda. Carly waved as she and Captain jogged past the old mansion and headed for the stable and corrals.

"Finally!" Luke called from inside the nearest corral. Carly could see he already had two barrels set up and ready to go. "I was just about to start without you." He rolled the third oil drum into place and set it upright.

"Sorry." Carly pulled Captain to a halt next to Luke's Buckskin marc, Sunny. The tan-colored mare nickered at Captain and shook her head in welcome. He returned the greeting by nuzzling Sunny's neck.

"Can I ride, too?" asked Luke's little sister, Josie. The seven-year-old was perched on the top rail of the fence, holding Sunny's reins.

"Not today," Luke said. "Carly and I have a lot of work to do if we want to be ready for the Play Day on Sunday."

"Ignore him, Squirt," Carly said. "You can ride Captain if you want."

"Thanks." Josie stuck out her tongue at Luke.

"Spoiled brat," he muttered.

"What did you say?" Carly asked.

"I called Josie a spoiled brat. Why? Did you think I was talking about you?"

"I'm not spoiled."

"Sure you are." Luke took off his western straw hat and wiped his forehead with the sleeve of his shirt. "An only kid. Nobody messing with your things or begging to ride your horse. You're the spoiledest kid I know."

"Look who's talking. The boy who lives in a castle, for heaven's sake!" Carly slid off Captain's back. She untied her spurs from the back of the saddle and fastened them to the heels of her boots.

"How many times do I have to tell you. It's not a castle—it just looks like one!" Luke scrambled over the fence and grabbed Sunny's reins from Josie. Hooking the stirrup over the pommel of his saddle, he checked the cinch strap to make sure it was tight. "And don't try to change the subject. We were talking about you, not me."

"Well, if I'm the spoiledest kid you know, then you must not know Savannah Winters," Carly said. "Now there's a spoiled kid!"

"Annie doesn't count. She's a city kid. And all city kids are spoiled."

"That's true. But she has to be the worst. You should have heard her bragging at the grain elevator's picnic last month." Carly raised her voice an octave and wiggled her hips. "How do you like my new jeans? Look at this watch I got for my birthday. Do you want to see the pictures we took at the Grand Canyon?"

"She's not that bad," Luke said, laughing.

"She is, too. And you should see that Arabian mare her grandpa bought her!" Carly shook her head in amazement. "Buttercup's Princess. A princess for a princess, he told my dad."

"He didn't really say that, did he?"

"He did. I almost threw up when I heard it."

"Luke! Carly! Are you two going to yak all day?" Josie asked.

"Maybe," Luke replied.

"Not me," Carly said "I'm going to run the barrels!" She climbed back into the saddle and guided Captain toward the open gate of the corral. *You control the race. Only you. Make sure Captain is in position before you start.* Grandpa's familiar words echoed in her head, as if he was sitting right behind her, whispering in her ear. Carly gathered Captain's leather reins in both hands and pointed Captain toward the barrels. Then, with a click of her tongue and a flick of her spurs, they were off.

They were almost to the first barrel when Carly

pulled on the reins. Leaning slightly to the right, she guided Captain into a tight turn. As soon as they were past the barrel, Carly dug in her spurs and the big sorrel surged ahead.

"Go, Carly, go!"

Carly grinned when she heard Josie's voice. It was great to have her own personal cheering section. Carly could just imagine the scowl on Luke's face. She laughed.

Suddenly, they were at the second barrel. Once again, Carly tugged on the reins. This time, though, her timing was off. She felt a sharp pain in her left knee as it grazed the metal edge. They left the barrel rocking and Carly heard Josie squeal.

Carly wanted to look back, but she knew she couldn't afford to waste even a second. *Every time you enter the ring, you ride like this is for the championship. Practice or real; it makes no never-mind.* Carly knew Grandpa was right. She urged Captain forward and he circled the barrel without touching it.

Carly stood up in the stirrups and leaned over the saddle horn. Her hands almost touched Captain's ears as she loosened the reins and raced for the finish line. She pulled Captain to an abrupt halt at the gate of the corral. Then she gave in to temptation and looked back at the second barrel. It had withstood its rocky ride and was still standing.

"18.1 seconds. Great run," Luke called. He sat on top of Sunny, stopwatch in hand.

"Yeah," Josie said. "You and Captain are the best!"

"Hey, wait a minute." Luke glared at his sister. "What about Sunny and me? What are we?"

"The worst!" she said. Luke took a stab at her with his leather baton, but Josie jumped down from the fence and ran for the safety of their front yard.

"Coward!" Luke called, before turning his attention back to Carly. "She's right, though. You two look mighty good out there."

"Thanks. I'm just happy the second barrel didn't go down."

"It should have. You clipped it pretty hard."

"You don't have to tell me." Carly reached down and rubbed her knee. "My leg is killing me! I bet it'll be black and blue for a week."

"Probably. Maybe you should get some of those knee guards, like Annie wears."

"I'm not wearing no sissy knee guards! Like Grandpa says, it's a long way from my heart. Now, are you going to ride, or as Josie says, are you going to keep 'yakking' about my leg?" Carly held out her hand.

"I'm going, I'm going." Luke placed the stopwatch in Carly's outstretched palm.

Carly watched Luke's ride with interest. Sunny was not a natural performer in the arena, and last year she'd fought Luke at every barrel. But not today. Today, Luke had the mare completely in control and Sunny's turns were smooth, though still too wide.

"Well?" Luke asked, pulling up next to Carly.

"19.3. Not bad. You ride like this on Sunday and Captain and I may actually have some competition!"

"Thanks!" Luke sighed and patted Sunny's neck. "But it still isn't as good as I'd hoped. We just can't seem to break into the 18s."

"My turn, my turn," Josie called, as she skipped across the dirt path toward the corral.

"You don't get a turn. Remember?" Luke asked.

"Yes, she does," said Carly. "Remember?" She jumped down and handed the reins to Josie.

"Yeah! I like Captain better than Sunny, anyway."

Carly laughed. "Me, too!" She hoisted Josie into the saddle. "Wait a minute," she said. "If you're going to run the barrels, you need your stirrups set right." Carly shortened the straps on each side. "How does that feel?"

Josie stood up in the saddle to test the length. "Perfect!"

"Great, Squirt. Show Luke how a real rider does it!"

Luke snorted. "If she beats my time, I'll . . . I'll . . . Well, I don't know what I'll do, but it won't be funny!"

Josie laughed. "Yes, it will!" She steered Captain toward the open gate.

"I'm ready!" Josie called from inside the arena.

"Go!" When Carly gave the signal, Josie kicked Captain in both sides. He took off at a trot for the first barrel, and Carly grinned at Luke. "I don't think you have to worry about her beating your time today. With Josie on his back, Captain won't go much faster than one of those ponies on a merry-go-round."

"That's true," Luke said. "He is one special horse. Your grandpa sure knows how to pick them."

"Yeah, he does. Or, at least he did." Carly leaned her elbows on the middle bar of the corral fence.

"How is he?" Luke slipped off Sunny's back to join her.

"Not good. Ever since his stroke, he can't walk or talk Mom says he still knows everybody, but I don't it's true."

Carly stopped. She looked down at the ground and kicked a dirt clod. She knew if she kept talking, she'd start to blubber like a baby. And that was something she never did. Not in front of Luke. Not in front of anybody.

The two watched as Josie carefully circled the second barrel. Then Luke asked, "What's going to happen to him?"

"I don't know. Grandma wants him to move home once he's better, but Mom says Grandma isn't strong enough to take care of him. Not by herself, anyway. Mom hasn't said so, but I think she wants Grandma and Grandpa to move to the farm and live with us."

Carly straightened as Josie rounded the last barrel and headed Captain toward home. She pressed the button on the stopwatch as the team trotted past her.

"Good ride, Squirt," she called. "28.6. I think that's the first time you've broken into the twenties! You just keep getting better with every ride!"

Carly turned to Luke. "I'd like to beat you one more time, but Mom is helping Grandma in Lincoln again, so there's no one but me to do the chores. And I think I hear Rosie calling. If I don't get home and milk her soon, she'll probably explode."

"Carly, cows don't explode!" Josie said. She slipped down from the saddle, and Carly readjusted the stirrups once more.

"I hope you're right, Squirt. But I don't want to take any chances."

"Hey, Carly," Luke said. "I was just thinking. If your mom gets her wish, you'll be just like Annie—a spoiled girl, living with her grandpa."

Carly grabbed Luke by the arms. She pushed him up against the fence. "Take it back," she demanded. "Take it back!"

Josie grabbed Luke by the legs, and between them, they wrestled him to the ground.

"Hey, two against one," he yelled. "No fair!"

"Say you're sorry! Say you didn't mean it!" Carly repeated, as Josie started to tickle him.

"I'm . . . sorry," Luke said, laughing and wriggling to get loose. "I . . . didn't . . . mean . . . it."

Carly loosened her grip and stood up. She brushed the dirt off her denim jeans and scowled down at Luke. "Well, I do mean it," she said. "Don't you ever say anything like that again. I'm nothing like Savannah Winters, and I never will be!" Then, without saying another word, she climbed into the saddle and galloped for home.

Chapter 2
The Surprise

Carly's anger melted as Captain galloped down the gravel road toward home, and by the time she reached the entrance to their lane, her fight with Luke was all but forgotten. Angel, her German Shepherd, waited for Carly under a cottonwood tree. As soon as Angel caught sight of her, she barked twice, then dashed up the dusty road ahead of them. Carly laughed and tugged slightly on the reins. She wanted to give Angel the head start she needed to beat them back to the barn.

And it worked. By the time they cantered into the farmyard, Angel was waiting at the barn door. She barked twice more, then sat on her haunches while Carly dismounted. The minute Carly was on the ground, though, Angel was on her feet again, barking and jumping in front of her.

"Did you miss me?" Carly asked. She reached down and scratched behind the dog's ears.

"Miss you?" Dad asked as he rounded the corner of the barn with a bucket of milk. He set the bucket down and stretched his arms wide. "I sure did! And what about you? Did you miss me?"

"Dad! You're home!" Carly ran and gave him a hug. "But why are you here so early?" Her dad worked at the grain elevator in the city twenty miles away, and he rarely got home before six o'clock.

"I wanted to surprise you. Since this is your first day of summer and your mom is coming home for the weekend, I thought we should have a celebration. You finish the chores and I'll go rustle us up something for supper." Dad snapped his fingers and Angel immediately came to attention. "Come on, Girl. Follow me." He picked up the bucket of milk and headed for the house, Angel dancing at his side.

Carly tied Captain's reins to the corral fence so she could unsaddle him. Then she stored the blanket and saddle in the barn's tack room, grabbed the currycomb, and hurried back outside.

"Just a lick and promise tonight, Boy. Sorry." Carly ran the comb over Captain's rust-red coat. Tomorrow, when she had more time, she would give Captain a proper grooming, including trimming his hooves and combing his tail. The Carsten Castle Play Day was the first official horse show of the season, and she wanted him to look perfect.

Carly closed her eyes as she stroked Captain's mane and imagined the editor of the Riley Weekly Gazette taking their picture for the front page of the newspaper, while she proudly held the championship barrel racing trophy in her hand.

A loud "Moo!" snapped her out of her daydream. Rosie stood by the feeding trough next to the fence, bawling and shaking her head.

Carly laughed. "I'm coming. I'm coming," she said. "Though I don't know how you can still be hungry. I know you were eating the whole time Dad milked you!"

She turned Captain into the corral, then grabbed an alfalfa bale from a stack by the barn wall. She carried it to the fence and tipped it over the top rail. As it fell, Carly pulled the strings and the hay tumbled into the trough. Rosie immediately stopped her bawling and began to eat. Captain, though, waited patiently while Carly spread the hay evenly in the box, before he, too, joined Rosie at the trough.

Next, Carly filled a metal bucket with chicken feed and another bucket with water from the pump. She climbed the hill to the little shed that housed their chickens, trying not to slosh the water on her boots. As she walked, she thought about how nice it was not to have to milk tonight.

It wasn't that Carly didn't like to milk. She did. She loved the smell of the warm, fresh milk mingled with the musty odor of the barn hay. She loved to hear the twang the streams of milk made as they first hit the side of the metal bucket, and how that sound changed as the bucket began to fill. She even loved the way the barn cats all came running when they heard that sound, and how they begged to be given a shot of the warm milk, right from the teat.

But milking was time-consuming, and it wasn't her job, plain and simple. Ever since Carly was little, the McCallister family had divided the chores evenly. Dad took care of all the farm and house repairs, like fixing the cistern or painting the house, and all the machinery chores, like mowing the lawn and grinding the feed.

Mom was supposed to milk Rosie and take care of most of the inside chores, like cooking and cleaning. Except, of course, for Carly's room. Cleaning her room and feeding the animals were Carly's jobs.

But ever since Grandpa Meyer had his stroke, nothing was like it was supposed to be. Mom was always helping Grandpa and Grandma in Lincoln. Dad was always working extra hours at the grain elevator. And Carly was stuck at home, doing all the chores. It just wasn't fair.

Carly wondered what Dad was fixing for supper. Something easy, that was for sure. Dad wasn't much of a cook. Carly didn't care what it was. Like Rosie, she was starved and would eat almost anything. Her stomach rumbled just to prove the point.

The minute Carly walked through the doorway, she could smell hamburger browning on the stove. She peeked under the lid of the frying pan. Sloppy joe loose meats! Carly grinned. Dad knew they were her favorite. Especially the way he made them, with lots of ketchup and brown sugar. Served hot on Mom's home-made bread, sloppy joes were the best. She kicked off her boots and headed to the sink to wash her hands.

"Carly, can you set the table?" Dad asked. His back was to her and he was digging around in the closet pantry. "Your mom will be here any minute, and I'm still trying to figure out what we're going to eat for dessert."

"Sure." Carly grabbed plates from the cupboard and silverware from the drawer. She was just placing the last fork on the table when Mom walked in.

"How's Grandpa?" Carly asked.

"The same," Mom said with a sigh. "No better. No worse." She collapsed onto one of the chairs at the kitchen table. "Though it's your grandma I'm really worried about. She just isn't taking care of herself. She's not cooking or cleaning or going out. It's like she doesn't know what to do with herself, now that Grandpa isn't there."

Dad came over and put his hand on her shoulder. "It will all work out. You'll see." He smiled and gave Carly a wink. "Now, let's sit down and eat. I can't wait for you to try my newest creation. I added a secret ingredient that I think you're both going to love."

"Oh, no, Dad, you didn't!" Carly groaned. "You know I hate surprises."

"Now, Carly, my girl. It's the surprises that make

life interesting. If we knew what was around every corner, there'd be no reason to keep walking. Take each day as it comes and enjoy the journey. That's what my daddy used to say."

Even though her dad was talking to her, Carly could tell the words were really meant for her mom. He was trying to cheer her up. "Okay," Carly said. "I'll eat it. But I'm not promising to like it!"

Dad laughed. "Fair enough. Now, both of you sit down. I have some important news I want to share."

Carly looked at Mom, but she only shrugged her shoulders. "What is it, Dad?" Carly asked. "Are you getting a raise?"

"I guess you could say that," he said. "It does involve making more money." Dad paused and looked at Carly. "I've been offered a job as manager at a grain elevator in Lincoln."

"Oh, Ray, that's wonderful!" Mom clapped her hands over her heart. "Are you absolutely sure, though?" she asked.

Dad nodded and smiled. "Yep. Mr. Meeks, the owner, called today and asked how soon I could start." Dad stopped and took a deep breath. "I've been thinking about it all day. If we get busy, we should have the place ready for auction by the middle of July and be settled in Lincoln by August 1."

Carly stared at her parents. "Auction? What are you talking about?"

Ray McCallister cleared his throat. "You heard me, Carly. We're selling the farm and moving to Lincoln."

Carly gasped. "No!" she shouted. "I don't believe you. You would never make us leave Riley!"

Dad looked at Mom across the table, then back at Carly. "I know this comes as a shock to you. But Mom and I've been thinking about moving for a while. And we think living in Lincoln is our best option."

"What do you mean, best? Best for who? Not me. That's for sure."

"Best for all of us, young lady, including you. A year from now, you'll be going into the seventh grade. There's no question that you'll have more opportunities in Lincoln than you have in Riley. Plus, your grandpa and grandma need us. And we need to be there, for them."

"But what about the animals?" Carly asked. "What will happen to them?"

"We'll take Angel with us. As for Rosie and the

chickens, I'll put an ad in the paper next week. If they don't sell by mid-July, then we'll just have to include them in the farm sale. The cats are as much a part of this place as the row of windbreak trees and the outbuildings. Whoever buys the place will just inherit them, I guess."

"What about Captain?" Carly asked. "You forgot Captain."

Her dad sighed. And she knew. This bad news was about to get worse.

"I spoke with Mr. Winters about that today," Dad said. "He's starting to think that Arabian mare he bought for Savannah is too high-strung to use for rodeo competition. He's looking for the best show horse his money can buy, and he thinks Captain might just be that horse." Dad rested his calloused hands on Carly's shoulders and looked her in the eyes. "So the two of us made a deal. I told him if we move to Lincoln, we'll sell Captain to him."

Carly gasped. She couldn't believe it. Captain was her horse. Grandpa had bought him for her. Dad didn't have the right to sell him. Not to Jasper Winters. Not to anyone.

Carly jumped up and her chair toppled behind her.

"I won't let you do it," she screamed. "Captain is mine. All mine. And nobody will ever take him away from me!" Then she turned and ran out of the room.

Chapter 3
The Plan

Carly flipped over on her side and looked at the clock. 5:30 in the morning and she was still awake! She might as well get up. She wasn't going to sleep. How could she? Not when the conversation with Dad kept playing in her head.

She shuffled to the window and pushed the curtains aside. The barnyard lamp flooded the corral in light, and Carly's eyes immediately sought out Captain. He was standing next to the fence, looking at the house. She wondered if he could see her. Suddenly, she had the overwhelming need to bury her face in his soft warm coat.

She grabbed her jeans from the floor of her closet and shimmied into them. She tip-toed down the stairs and sidled past her parents' room, trying not to wake them. But it didn't work.

"Carly?" her mom called. "What are you doing?"

"I couldn't sleep, so I thought I'd get up and do my chores."

Carly heard the soft mixture of her parents' voices, but she couldn't make out the words. Then finally, her dad's voice. "Okay, Carly. Thanks."

Carly expected him to say he'd get up to help her, but he didn't. She was glad. She didn't want to talk to him. She just wanted to spend some time alone, with Captain.

She escaped out the back door. The screen door slammed behind her and Carly shrugged. There was no reason to be quiet now.

Carly breathed in the cool morning air. The sun was just beginning to rise above the pasture, and the morning sky was a mixture of oranges and pinks and purples. Grandpa used to say that dawn was his favorite time of day. It always looked to him like someone had tipped over the pastel paint jars in heaven and was trying desperately to clean up the mess before the big guy found out.

Carly smiled at the memory. When she was little,

she never knew who Grandpa was talking about when he said "the big guy." The only big guy she knew was Santa Claus, and he lived at the North Pole, not in heaven. It wasn't until she was at Sunday School one morning that she figured out who Grandpa was really talking about.

A lick on her hand brought her back to the present. "Good morning, Angel," Carly said. She got down on her knees and gave the dog a proper hug. "How did you sleep?"

Angel barked and wagged her tail.

"Lucky you!" Carly said. "I had a terrible night's sleep." As she scratched behind the dog's ears, she continued the conversation. "Did you hear about Dad's 'surprise'? We're moving, Angel. To Lincoln! Can you believe it?"

Angel whined, sat down on her haunches, and tipped her head to stare up at Carly.

"Don't fret, Angel. At least you'll be coming with us. It's Captain that's in trouble." Carly stood up and clicked her fingers. "Come on. I want to tell him the bad news myself, before he hears it from somebody else." Angel barked and immediately stood up, then followed Carly to the corral. Grandpa would be so proud of Angel, Carly thought. Carly and Grandpa had worked with her all winter, trying to get her to respond to commands. Now, the pup knew every command by heart.

As Carly crossed the farmyard, headed for the corral, she wondered how she was going to break the news to Captain. Although she knew that Luke didn't agree with her, she was sure that her animals understood every word she said. And she didn't want to just spring this on him, like Dad had sprung it on her.

But then, maybe that was best, sort of like pulling a bandage off your arm. Sometimes it was better to just rip it off and deal with the pain all at once, instead of pulling it a little bit at a time and prolonging the process.

Carly clambered up the fence. She straddled the top and looked down at Angel. "Stay." Then she jumped off the fence and into the corral.

Captain met her halfway. He nosed her pocket. "No treat today, Captain," she said. "But I'll bring something next time, I promise." She looked him straight in the eyes as she ran her hand up and down his nose. "Cap, I have something to tell you." She took a deep breath and then plunged ahead. "Dad says we have to sell the farm and Rosie and you, so we can move to Lincoln and take care of Grandpa and Grandma."

Captain closed his eyes, like he couldn't believe what she was saying.

"I know it sounds bad, but I don't want you to worry. Because he's wrong. He has to be. Somehow, someway, I'm going to find a way to take you with me. I promise!"

Carly buried her face into the side of Captain's neck. And for the first time since Grandpa's stroke, she let herself cry. Really cry. Not silent drops running down her cheeks in the middle of the night, but one great big salty stream of tears that rolled into her mouth and soaked Captain's coat. And the harder she cried, the tighter she squeezed Captain's neck. But he didn't seem to mind. He stood there and let her cry— just like she knew he would.

Finally, the tears slowed. She forced herself to let go of Captain and wiped her nose and eyes with the back of her hand. "Sorry about that, Cap," she said with a hiccup. "I'm okay now."

He looked at her with his soft brown eyes. Carly

tried to imagine never looking into those eyes again, or burying her face in his neck, and she couldn't do it. She wouldn't do it!

Carly's thoughts were interrupted by a low "Mooo." Carly laughed, though the sound came out shaky. "No, Rosie, I haven't forgotten you. And I know what time it is. Come on. Let's get you milked and fed."

While Carly milked Rosie, she shared Dad's news one more time. Only this time, she didn't make any promises. It would be hard enough to convince her folks to take Captain to Lincoln. It would be impossible to keep both animals in the city. Carly felt guilty, knowing that she wouldn't miss Rosie in the same way that she'd miss Captain. But she knew that Rosie understood. And Dad would choose Rosie's next owner carefully. Wouldn't he?

Carly rested her chin on Rosie's back as she milked. Rosie's coat was short and scratchy, like a scouring pad, but Carly ignored the sensation. She squeezed her swollen, tear-soaked eyelids tight and tried to concentrate on the job at hand. In her mind, she could picture Grandpa sitting next to her, joking, "This is a job you've done so often, you can do it with your eyes closed."

"I wish Grandpa was here, right now," Carly told Rosie. "He'd tell me what to do." But he wasn't. And if he was here, there wouldn't be a problem, because they wouldn't be moving to Lincoln to take care of him. Carly sighed. Why did everything have to be so complicated?

As soon as she was done milking, she took Rosie back to the corral and filled the trough with hay. Then she trudged to the house with the bucket of fresh milk.

Carly followed her nose to the kitchen and set the bucket of fresh milk on the kitchen counter. She watched as Mom pulled a batch of cinnamon rolls from the oven. The kitchen smelled of dough and cinnamon and sugar and her mom hummed along to some song on the radio, as if she didn't have a care. Carly wondered how that could be, when their whole world was falling apart.

"Thanks for milking, Carly. You wash up while I take care of it," Mom said. "Dad's out in the shed, changing the oil on the car. As soon as he comes in, we'll eat."

"I'm not hungry. I'm going to call Luke."

"Carly, we need to talk about the move to Lincoln."

"Why? Dad said we're moving. Unless he's changed

his mind, there isn't much more to say, is there?"

"Carly!"

She could hear the hurt and frustration in Mom's voice, but Carly didn't care. She turned her back and marched across the room to the phone. Luke's mom answered on the third ring.

"Carly, hi. How's your grandpa?"

"Not so good. He's still in the nursing home."

"Such a shame. He was always so active."

"Yeah, I know. It stinks." Carly took a deep breath. She hated talking about Grandpa. She hated thinking about him, sitting in that nursing home, when he should be here, sitting at the kitchen table, playing Double Solitaire with her while Grandma and Mom gossiped about a lot of nothing.

"You let your folks know if they need anything, all they have to do is ask." Mrs. Carsten's voice interrupted her thoughts.

"Thanks, Mrs. C. I will. Can I talk to Luke?" Carly asked.

"I'm sorry, Carly. He's not here. He's down at the creek, fishing. Do you want me to have him call when he gets back?"

"No, thanks. I'll just ride down there and find him."

Carly hung up the phone and headed for the door.

"Carly, you have to eat," Mom said. "Here, take these with you."

Carly stopped and turned around. Mom was wrapping some cinnamon rolls in aluminum foil. She set the package on the counter and opened her arms. Carly hesitated, then slipped into them. Her mom held her tight, but didn't say a word. Carly was glad. Sometimes a hug was better than words.

Finally, Carly backed away. "I better get going. I don't want to miss Luke."

"I'll tell Dad where you are. Don't stay at the creek too long."

"I won't." Carly took the rolls from the counter and headed for the back porch. Her saddlebag and water bottle, presents from Grandpa and Grandma, were hanging next to each other on metal pegs. She stuffed the rolls into the leather pouch and swung it over her shoulder. Then she grabbed the metal bottle. She'd fill it outside at the water pump.

The garage door was closed and Dad was nowhere in sight. Carly saddled Captain as quickly as she could. She wanted to be gone before Dad saw her. She knew Mom wouldn't force her to talk, but he might. And she needed to see Luke before that happened. She needed someone to be on her side.

As Captain trotted down the road, Carly thought about Dad's "surprise." How could he do this? How could he sell their farm and their animals? How could he sell Captain?

That's when it hit her. Dad said he was taking out newspaper ads to find homes for Rosie and the chickens. But if Dad could take out an ad, so could she! Dad said they couldn't afford to take Captain with them to Lincoln. But there had to be a farm somewhere close to Lincoln where she could keep Captain for free, in exchange for doing chores. All she had to do was find that place.

But how could she run an ad in the newspaper without her parents knowing about it? How would she pay for the ad? Would she have to give a phone number? Whose phone number would she give? She couldn't give their number. What would she say if someone called and Mom or Dad answered the phone?

The questions tumbled over each other in her head. Carly had never put an ad in a newspaper before. She wasn't even sure how to do it. She knew she'd need help. But who could she ask? Not Luke. He was smart, but Carly was pretty sure he wouldn't know any more about newspaper ads than she did.

But Grandma Meyer would! Every year, her grandmother asked her what she wanted for her birthday. And every year, Carly said the same thing. "I don't know, Grandma. Get me whatever you want."

But not this year. This year, she would ask Grandma to help her take out a newspaper ad in the Lincoln paper. Grandma knew how important Captain was to Grandpa and her.

But would Grandma agree to keep it a secret from Mom and Dad? Carly didn't know about that. Did it really need to be a secret? What if Carly just asked her mom and dad to take out the ad? No, that was too risky. What if they said no? Then, if she did it anyway, she would be deliberately disobeying them and asking her grandma to do the same.

But once it was done and Carly had a place to keep Captain, what could her parents say? They would have to let her take Captain to Lincoln!

By the time Carly reached the creek, she had it all worked out in her head. She found Luke sitting on the bank, fishing pole in the water. There was no sign of Sunny, so Carly figured he must have walked.

Carly tied Captain's reins to a nearby tree. She dug the cinnamon rolls out of her saddlebag. They were still warm. Then she headed for the bank and Luke.

"Any bites?" she asked, as she dropped down next to him.

"Nope, not yet," Luke said. "But it's early."

"I brought breakfast. Fresh from the oven." Carly unwrapped the package of rolls and set it down on the ground between them. They were a bit squished but Carly knew Luke wouldn't care.

"Wow! Thanks. I'm starved!" He grabbed one and gobbled it down. "Mm-mmm! Nobody makes rolls like your mom!" He reached for another one. But his hand hovered over them, stopping in midair. "How come you're not eating?" he asked, frowning. "What's wrong with them?"

"Nothing," Carly said. "I'm just not hungry."

"Okay. If you say so." Luke shrugged his shoulders, stuffed another roll into his mouth, and turned back toward the creek.

Carly watched his red and white bobber float on top of the water. Now that she was here, she wasn't sure how to start. Finally, she just blurted it out. "We're moving."

"What?" Luke mumbled, his mouth full of roll. He swallowed, then squinted over his shoulder at Carly. "What did you say?"

"Us. My mom and dad and me. We're moving to Lincoln."

Luke dropped his pole and scrambled to his feet. "You can't be!"

"We are. Dad told us last night. We're moving there in August."

"Why?"

"So we can live with Grandma Meyer and help her take care of Grandpa."

"That's terrible!"

"Yeah, but that's not even the worse part."

"What could be worse than moving?" Luke asked.

"Selling everything. Rosie. The chickens." Carly went through the list of things that she'd lose, her voice getting softer and softer. "The farm." By the time she reached the end, she was whispering. "Captain." In fact, she wasn't even sure she had actually said Captain's name out loud. But from the look on Luke's face, she must have.

"Your dad is selling Captain?" He looked as stunned as Carly had been when she first heard the news.

"Yes, to Savannah Winters' grandpa! Can you believe it?"

"No, I can't. I didn't think your folks would ever sell Captain." He stared down at the water. Then, almost as if he was talking to himself, he said, "It's too bad my dad didn't know Captain was for sale. I bet he would have bought him for Josie."

Carly couldn't believe her ears. How dare Luke even suggest such a thing! "Captain is not for sale!"

"But you just said—"

"I know what I said. But I'm not going to let that happen!"

"And just how are you going to stop it?"

"I have a plan." Quickly, Carly outlined her idea. When she was finished, she grinned at Luke, waiting for him to tell her how brilliant it was.

But Luke wasn't smiling.

"What's wrong?" she asked.

"I don't know, Carly. Mr. Winters is your dad's boss. Do you really think your dad will back out of the deal, after he's given his word?"

"Whose side are you on?" Carly asked. She untied Captain's reins and climbed into the saddle.

"This isn't about choosing sides," Luke protested.

"This is about your plan. Which I don't think is going to work."

"You're wrong," Carly shouted over her shoulder as she and Captain galloped away from the creek. "He is wrong," Carly assured Captain as she leaned over the saddle and rubbed his neck. "It will work, Boy! I know it will. You just wait and see."

Chapter 4
The Cave

Once she rounded the bend of the creek, Carly tugged on the reins. There was no reason to hurry. As soon as she got home, Mom and Dad would just put her to work. She might as well go riding instead. If Dad had his way, Captain would belong to Savannah Winters in August, but for right now Captain was still her horse, and she would ride him every chance she got.

A drop of water landed on her arm and another on her leg. Carly squinted at the morning sky. The clouds had changed from cotton balls to gray billows of smoke, and it was beginning to sprinkle. "Whoa, Captain. Those clouds look a little scary." Carly considered riding in the rain but decided against it. She sighed. "Come on, Boy. Let's head for home. If we're lucky, maybe we'll get there before we get too wet."

Carly and Captain galloped into their lane just as the clouds burst open and the shower turned into a downpour. Carly pulled up next to Mom, who was struggling to take the last two shirts off the clothesline.

"Carly, I'm glad you're home. I was just getting ready to send Dad out to look for you," Mom said. "We're in a severe thunderstorm warning. So we're going to sit this one out in the cave."

"Where's Dad?"

"He's closing up the chicken coop."

Carly nodded, then headed for the barn. She unsaddled Captain as quickly as she could, then wiped both him and the saddle dry before turning him into his stall.

Thunder rolled overhead and shook the walls of the old barn. Rosie stood in the stall next to Captain, chewing her cud. "Nothing ever bothers you, does it, Girl?" Carly asked, as she gave the old cow a pat on her neck. "I guess you've seen it all a hundred times before." She turned and headed for the door. "You two stay safe. I'll be back as soon as this storm blows over."

Carly stepped out of the barn and let loose a shrill whistle. Angel crawled out from under the porch steps.

As soon as she saw Carly, she barked and ran circles around her. "Sorry, Girl. I know you want to play. But I'm getting soaked. We need to get to the cave."

The rain pellets were sharp as they pummeled Carly's head and body, and the path was slick beneath her feet. She slipped and slid her way to their underground storm shelter, splattering mud on both Angel and herself.

A slanted wooden door on hinges protected the entrance to the storm shelter. Dad kept the hinges well oiled, and on calm days Carly had no trouble swinging the door open. But today the wind and rain fought against her. It took all her strength and both hands to lift it. Angel dashed ahead of her down the cement stairs, but Carly was more cautious. Even with the door open wide, she couldn't see a thing.

She waited for her eyes to adjust before creeping down the cement steps. Her fingers lightly trailed along the brick walls, guiding her way. At the base of the stairs, a small door protected the tiny underground room her parents called "the cave." Carly pushed it open and Angel rushed inside.

Carly waved her arms above her, blindly searching for the string to the bare lightbulb attached to the ceiling. Where was it? It should be here, right above her head.

Something grazed the side of her cheek. Was it the string or something else? Carly shivered and reached for that something, trying not to think about what else it could be. Her fingers brushed the string but could not capture it. It swung out of her grasp.

Angel barked and the sound echoed off the walls of the cave. "I know, Girl. I'm working on it. Be patient!" Carly reached above her head once more and slowly waved her arms in a circle above her head. Her right palm connected with the string once more, and Carly quickly closed her fist around it and pulled. Light flooded the small room. Carly let go of the breath she hadn't realized, until then, she was holding. What was it about light that instantly made her feel safer?

The brick walls of the cave were lined with wooden shelves. Each shelf was packed with canning jars of all shapes and sizes, filled with pickles and tomatoes and a variety of fruit preserves and jams. On the floor of the cave, under the shelves, were large stoneware kegs, covered in dust and cobwebs. Carly wasn't sure how long they'd been there or what was in them. She knew for a fact her mom had never touched them.

Angel seemed particularly interested in those kegs. Every couple of minutes she would stop sniffing and bark at them, then return to sniffing. Carly wondered if Angel had really found something or if the pup was just being overly curious. She considered checking it out for herself but decided against it. Carly wasn't too afraid of mice or spiders, but if there was a snake in the shelter with them, she didn't want to know about it.

Carly turned her back on Angel's snooping and headed for the old wooden chest and the three camping stools that were stored against the back wall.

Carly set the camping stools up in the center of the cave. Then she lifted the lid of the chest, took out a radio, and set it on the floor. Finally, she pulled out an old quilt and shook it, wrinkling her nose at the musty odor. Wrapping the quilt around her shoulders, Carly settled herself on one of the stools.

Angel barked at Carly from her spot in the corner. "Sorry, Girl. I'm not going over there. You come here." She whistled, and the pup trotted over to her. Angel plopped down next to Carly and rested her head in Carly's lap. Carly laughed and scratched Angel behind the ears. Then she switched on the radio. The local weatherman's voice echoed off the walls. "Again, I repeat. This storm is accompanied by high winds and dangerous lightning. Seek shelter immediately."

Carly heard the cave door slam shut and footsteps on the cement stairs.

"Hi, Carly! Looks like you got home just in time," Dad said from the door of the cave. "Mom was getting nervous. She was about to send out the posse!"

"I'm sorry," Carly said. "I hope Luke's okay."

"He's fine," Mom said, appearing right behind Dad. "His mom called to check on you. That's when I really started to worry."

While Carly and Dad continued to talk, Mom pulled two more quilts from the chest and handed one to Dad. Carly watched as her parents settled themselves on the stools next to her. Would this be the last time they ever had to wait out a storm in this dark, damp, cobwebby cave? A shiver of relief ran through her at the thought, but she quickly stomped it out. She refused to acknowledge there could be anything good about moving to Lincoln.

As if he'd read Carly's mind, Dad's voice cut through the silence. "Well, it looks like this storm has given us the one thing we needed most, time to talk. Who wants to go first?" He looked at both Mom and

Carly when he spoke, but Carly knew he was really talking to her.

Carly stared at her mud-splattered boots. She didn't want to talk about the move. Not now. Not ever. Why should she? What good would it do? Would they change their minds if she did talk? Could she change their minds? Carly peeked at them from shuttered eyes, hopeful. Maybe it wasn't a done deal. Maybe, if Mom and Dad were wanting to talk, they were willing to listen to her side and find another way to help Grandma and Grandpa, without selling the farm and moving to Lincoln.

Carly raised her head and stared first at her dad and then at her mom before speaking. "Why?" she asked. Her voice quivered and her hands shook. She cleared her throat and tried again. "Why are we moving? This is our home. This is where we're supposed to live."

"Carly, try to understand." Mom's soft voice seemed even softer than usual, as if the walls of the cave were swallowing the words as she spoke. "Grandpa is sick. Grandma's all alone in their big old house in Lincoln. They need me. And I need to be there for them. I know it doesn't seem fair to you. But it's the right thing to do. And it's what we're going to do."

"Why can't Grandpa and Grandma come here?" Carly asked. "We have lots of room. Why do we have to move to Lincoln?"

"Grandpa needs to be in the nursing home, at least for now. He has medical problems that Grandma and I just can't take care of by ourselves."

"Then he can stay there and Grandma can move." It was a horrible thing to say and Carly knew it. Even to her ears, the words sounded mean and selfish. But she couldn't take them back. She wouldn't!

"Carlene Louise," Dad said. Just that. Her name. But those two words were enough. Carly could hear the hurt and the disappointment, and she dropped her head and closed her eyes.

But when she pictured Captain, snorting and racing around the corral, the way he loved to do, she knew she couldn't give up that easily.

"Maybe if . . . isn't there some way we can take Captain with us?" Carly asked.

"I really wish we could," Mom said. "But we just don't have the kind of money it takes to board a horse in the city. Especially since we'd need a place that's close enough to Lincoln for you to get to every day."

"I've worked for Mr. Winters a long time and

known him even longer," Dad said. "He's a good man. He's paying us a fair price and he's willing to wait until the first of August to take possession. We can't ask any more than that."

"But what if he changes his mind?" Carly asked. "Can we take Captain to Lincoln then?

"He's not going to change his mind," Dad said. "You need to get that thought out of your head right now."

Mom put her arms around Carly and hugged her. "I know this is hard. It's hard for all of us. But if we stick together, we'll get through this. I promise."

Carly nodded but didn't say anything. After all, what was there to say? She leaned down and scratched Angel's ears. Mom took the hint and released her from the hug. Angel sighed and promptly fell asleep.

Carly wasn't sure how long the three of them sat there with only the sound of the radio announcer and Angel's slight snoring to keep them company. One hour. Two hours, maybe. Carly kept waiting for one of them to break the silence. Mom and Dad must have been waiting for the same thing, too, because no one did. It was like they were all frozen in time.

"The thunderstorm warning for Riley and the

surrounding area has ended." The weatherman's voice bounced off the walls of the cave, and just like that, the spell was broken.

"Not a moment too soon," Mom said. "I'm sure I felt a spider crawling up my arm!"

Carly watched as Mom stood, brushed herself from head to toe, and switched off the radio. Carly and her parents silently worked together to fold the three quilts and pack them in the chest, while Angel sat on her haunches, whining. When the quilts were stored, Mom settled the radio on top and closed the lid.

Angel dashed up the stairs, followed by Carly and her parents. Dad pushed open the hinged wooden door, and the family emerged, single-file. Except for the puddles of standing water and a few broken tree branches, scattered here and there in the yard, there was no real evidence that a storm had just passed their way.

"Good," Dad said. "I was worried about what was happening up here. But it looks like everything weathered the wind and rain just fine."

"Thank goodness," Mom said. "We already have enough to do. We don't need any extra messes to clean up."

"I'm going to check on Captain and Rosie," Carly said. As she trudged down the path to the barn, Angel prancing at her side, she thought back to the conversation in the cave. According to Mom and Dad, there wasn't anything she could do to stop Mr. Winters from buying Captain. But they were wrong. They had to be! Because there was no way she was moving to Lincoln without her horse.

Chapter 5
Letter to Grandpa

Dear Grandpa,

WHY? Why is this happening? Why did you have to get sick? Why did Grandma have to put you in that horrible place where everything smells like baby powder and bleach?

Carly stopped writing, stuck the end of the pen in her mouth, and chewed. When Grandpa had first gone to the nursing home, Carly wrote to him every day. But that had gradually slowed to once or twice a week. Now, it had been more than a month since her last letter to him.

Usually, the words came easy, but not today. So much had happened since the last time she wrote. She knew it wasn't Grandpa's fault they were moving to Lincoln. Not really.

But in her head, it was all jumbled up. If Grandpa hadn't gotten sick, Grandma wouldn't be living all alone. And if Grandma wasn't living all alone, Mom wouldn't be so worried about her. And if Mom wasn't so worried about Grandma, maybe they wouldn't have to sell the farm. Carly forced the pen back to the paper.

I'm scared, Grandpa. Scared of moving to the city. Scared of losing Captain. Scared of losing you. I want things to go back to the way they were. Back when all I had to do was wish upon a star, and my wish would magically come true.

Carly remembered the time she had wished for a puppy. The next week, she'd found a small gray bundle of fur in a basket on their back porch. She had scooped Angel into her arms. The pup barked, licked her chin, and Carly had fallen instantly in love.

Mom had said, "No. Absolutely not!" She didn't want a dog digging up her flowerbed or chasing the chickens.

"A girl needs a dog, Caroline," Grandpa had said.

"As I recall, when you were growing up, you didn't think the day was complete if you didn't get to spend some time down on the floor, scratching a dog's belly."

Carly could still see Mom, shaking her head and laughing. "Dad, you're a troublemaker," she had said. And Carly had known that Angel was hers.

Then there was the time Carly had been building a fort and accidentally left Dad's good hammer by the woodpile. By the time she remembered and went to find it, it was gone. She had dashed back to Dad's workshop and lifted the lid of his toolbox. There was the hammer, right where it was supposed to be.

I know that was you, Grandpa, making the magic happen. I need some of your magic, now. Please, Grandpa. Make it happen again.

Grandpa. She only had to close her eyes to see him. But not the way he was now, sitting in his wheelchair, hunched over, blanket tucked around his legs. He never smiled, and he looked through her, not at her. It was like he didn't even know Carly was there.

Grandpa would never have let Mom and Dad sell the farm and move to Lincoln. He would have known just what to say or do to fix this problem. But now, the way he was, he couldn't do or say anything.

Carly looked down at the letter in her hand. She knew Grandpa would not really be reading it. Not by himself. He couldn't. Grandma would read it to him when she came for her daily visit.

Carly pictured Grandma, picking up the letter from the nightstand. She'd open it with her nail file, the way she opened all of her mail. Then she would slide the notepaper out and start to read.

That's where Carly stopped. She couldn't imagine Grandma reading these words out loud. And even if she did, Carly knew that Grandpa wouldn't understand them. They would mean nothing to him.

Carly crumpled the paper and tossed it in the wastebasket. Taking out a clean sheet of notepaper, she wiped a tear, and began again.

Dear Grandpa,

How are you? The weather here is fine. A bit rainy, but that's good for the garden. The tomato vines are growing like weeds. Before you know it, they'll be filled with tomatoes.

The Carsten Castle Play Day is tomorrow.

Mrs. Hays went to a horse show in Ponca last summer, and she came back with some ideas for a whole bunch of new events. Besides the barrels and the poles, there's going to be a hat race and musical tires and something called Sandsurfing. Luke and I are going to be a team for that race. He has to try and stand up on a square piece of plywood while Captain and I pull him around the corral as fast as we can. Mrs. Hays says it is sort of like waterskiing on dry land. I think it sounds like lots of fun. I wish you could be there to see it.

Last time I saw Grandma, she asked me what I wanted for my birthday. Tell her I've been thinking about it and I have an idea. I'll talk to her about it the next time I see her. Well, I better get this to the mailbox so it can go out today.

Love always, Carly

Carly folded the paper into thirds and slipped it into the envelope. Turning the envelope over, she addressed it to Carl Meyer in care of the Countryside Care Center, Lincoln, Nebraska. Then she slipped on her boots and headed for the door.

Chapter 6
A New Plan

"Stop laughing!" Carly shouted. She tried to run away, but her legs wouldn't cooperate. Why? What was wrong with them?

She forced her eyes open. Her heart was hammering in her chest. She took deep gulps of air, trying to calm herself. Where was she? She looked around. She was in her own room, in her own bed. Carly struggled to sit up but she still couldn't move. Her legs were tangled in her quilted bedcover.

It was just a dream, she thought. Just a dream. She tried to recall the details. They came back in pieces, like a movie that was all mixed up.

She and Luke were standing by the carriage house at Carsten Castle. Josie was riding Captain and there was a crown perched on Captain's head, between his ears. Josie was shouting at them. She kept saying she was riding the king of the barrel racers. Luke was saying that Carly was just like Savannah. Mr. Winters had bought Savannah a princess of a horse and Carly's grandpa had bought her a king. Carly was trying to tell Luke he was wrong when she noticed that Josie wasn't riding Captain anymore. Now, Savannah was in the saddle and Mr. Winters was talking to Dad. He said he had come to trade a princess for a king. Then everyone started to laugh. Dad and Mr. Winters and Luke and Savannah—all of them laughing and pointing at Carly.

Carly fought to control her breathing. It was just a dream. Just a bad dream. But it wasn't. Not really. This was her life.

Luke said that Carly's dad would not go back on his word. Carly knew that it was true. But she wondered if the same could be said of Mr. Winters. Dad said Mr. Winters wanted the best horse he could buy for Savannah. At one time, he must have thought Buttercup's Princess was that horse. But he changed his mind about that, didn't he? Surely there was a way to make him change his mind about Captain, too.

Downstairs, Carly could hear the rattling of pots and pans and Mom singing. Carly's room was at the top of the stairs and the smell of sausages and hot maple syrup wafted temptingly up to her.

Carly shuffled to the window, yawning and stretching as she went. She pulled back the curtains and squinted at the yard below. Captain was rolling about in the pasture, taking a dust bath, while Rosie stood watching, chewing her cud.

"Carly, breakfast!" Mom's voice floated up the stairs.

"Just a minute," Carly said. "I'm not dressed yet." She grabbed a pair of jeans from the bottom drawer of her dresser. She was still snapping the buttons on her western plaid shirt as she clattered down the stairs.

"How do pancakes sound?"

"Great," Carly said. "I'm starved." She looked over at Dad's spot.

"He's already out the door," Mom said, even though Carly hadn't asked. "He said he would take care of the chores this morning, so you don't have to worry about them."

"Thanks, Mom."

"Don't thank me. Thank your dad." Mom smiled

as she picked up Dad's dishes. "And you better get moving. It's seven fifteen now. Didn't Mrs. Hays say she wanted all of you kids at the Carsten Estate by eight?"

"Yikes!" Carly grabbed two pancakes and a sausage. Stacking the pancakes, one on top of the other, she spread a thin layer of butter and syrup between each. Then she rolled them around the sausage and took a huge bite. Syrup dripped down her chin and over her fingers as she stuffed another chunk of the pancake-sausage roll into her mouth.

"Carly!" Mom scolded. "You're making a mess."

"Sorry, Mom. But like you said, I need to hurry," she mumbled, stuffing the last bit of pancakes and sausage into her mouth. She picked up her plate and set it on the counter, then rushed out the door.

By 7:40, she and Captain were on their way to Luke's and the annual Carsten Castle Play Day, which officially marked the end of school each year. As Carly rode, her mind returned, once again, to the problem of Mr. Winters. How was she going to convince Dad's boss that Captain was not the wonderful horse he thought he was? There must be a way! But what could it be?

Perhaps she could train Captain to rear the minute Savannah climbed into the saddle? Carly grinned as she envisioned Savannah sitting on the ground in a pile of sandburs, watching Captain as he raced away from her. But then Carly's smile faded. It would never work. Carly had trained Captain to rear while she was riding him, but he was too well behaved to act up with another rider on his back.

The sandburs got her to thinking, though. Maybe she could slip a handful of cockleburs under Captain's cinch, just as Savannah climbed into the saddle. That would make Captain kick and buck. Savannah would be on the ground before she could say "Stink and stank!" Carly laughed out loud thinking about it, but she knew she wouldn't do that either. She would never deliberately hurt Captain, not even to save him from Savannah Winters. No, there had to be another way.

What, in Mr. Winters' eyes, made Captain the perfect horse for Savannah? Carly thought back to last season and the county fair. That had been their best horse show, ever. They had taken first place in the barrels, the poles, and the obstacle course.

Later, Mr. Winters and Savannah had stopped by the horse barns to congratulate her. Captain's stall had been covered with purple ribbons. Mr. Winters had made a big deal of shaking her hand and telling her how much he'd enjoyed watching them perform, while Savannah just stood there, rubbing Captain's neck and not saying anything.

That was it! Mr. Winters wanted to buy Captain because of all those purple ribbons hanging on his stall. He wanted to own a winner, and Captain was the winningest horse he knew. But what if Captain started losing races instead of winning them?

Carly recalled their first practices in April, after the long winter. Even though she and Captain had been racing together for the past three summers, this spring Captain acted like he'd never run the pattern before. It had taken a good month to get him back to running smoothly.

And he still wasn't in perfect form. The bruise on her knee was proof of that. Of course, daily practice would soon solve that problem. But without daily practice, she and Captain would have trouble winning anything this year.

Carly sat up a little straighter in the saddle and grinned. "Come on, Cap," she said as she urged the big horse into a gallop. "We have a barrel race to lose!"

Chapter 7
Savannah Winters

When Carly reached the Carsten Castle, preparations for the Play Day were in full swing. Mrs. Hays, their teacher, called out orders and both kids and adults scurried to follow them. Everyone except Josie, that is.

"Carly. Over here." Josie sat cross-legged on the tailgate of the Carsten pickup truck, a peanut butter sandwich in one hand and a bottle of orange soda in the other.

Carly waved and steered Captain toward her.

"Mrs. Hays wants to see you right away," Josie said. "She needs someone to help at the registration table. It's set up by the Carriage House."

"Okay," Carly said. "I can do that. And what are you doing? Besides eating, of course."

"Mrs. Hays told me to keep an eye out for visitors so I can show them where to park and where to register. So, I'm waiting for them."

Carly hooked her left leg over the saddle horn, then shifted so she sat sidesaddle. "Where's Luke?"

"The last time I saw him, he was helping set up the obstacle course."

"Where's Flash?" Carly asked, looking around for Josie's Shetland pony. "Aren't you going to ride him today?"

"No," Josie said. "I wanted to, but Daddy says he's getting too old for horse shows anymore. And since Luke won't let me ride Sunny, I'm stuck just running the stupid footraces. Like a baby!"

"That stinks," Carly agreed. "There's nothing worse than being at a horse show without a horse!" She backed Captain away from the pickup, turned him around, and cantered off in the direction of the Carriage House.

As she rode, she wondered if she should tell Luke about her new plan to save Captain. She thought about his reaction when she'd told him she was going to run an ad in the Lincoln newspaper. All Luke did was come up with reasons why it wouldn't work.

Nope, Carly decided. She wasn't going to say a word, not to him or anyone else. She didn't want to know why this plan wouldn't work. Because it had to work! It just had to!

Suddenly, Carly felt a slap on her arm. "Yeouch!" she cried, startling Captain, who began to dance.

"Sorry," said Luke. "I didn't mean to scare you. I thought you heard us ride up."

Carly turned, but she couldn't believe her eyes. Perched on Sunny's rump, right behind Luke, sat Savannah Winters! Carly was so surprised she couldn't do anything but stare at them. Savannah was the last person she wanted to see.

"I told Luke that I wanted to talk to you, and since he was looking for you, too, he offered to give me a ride," Savannah said.

"Yeah, Luke's nice like that, isn't he?" Carly said, through gritted teeth.

Luke just shrugged.

"I wanted to tell you I'm sorry," Savannah said.

"About what?" Carly asked.

"About everything. About your grandpa being sick. About you having to move to Lincoln. About my family buying Captain."

"Yeah, well, it worked out good for you, didn't it?"

"Carly, it wasn't my idea. Really. I don't want a new horse. But Grandpa's stubborn. Once he decides on something, that's it. And he's decided he wants to sell Princess and buy Captain."

"All right, folks, it's time to get this year's Play Day underway." Mrs. Hays' voice boomed over the loudspeaker. "The first event of the day is the hat race. May I please see all of the contestants over by the judges' stand?"

Savannah smiled at Carly. "I just want you to know that I'll take real good care of Captain and you can come and ride him anytime you want. I promise. It'll be just like he's still your horse."

Carly's mouth dropped open. "What are you talking about? Things will never be the same again. Ever!" Carly twirled the big red sorrel in a circle away from Savannah and Luke. Completely ignoring their calls, she galloped Captain toward the arena and her first horse show of the season.

Chapter 8
The Play Day

Carly had always loved the Carsten Castle Play Day. It was meant to be a fun day, where the emphasis wasn't so much on winning as just having a good time.

But today, Carly was too worried about what would happen during the barrel race to enjoy the rest of the day. And to make matters worse, she couldn't decide if she should try to lose all the events she entered, or just that race.

As it turned out, she didn't have to worry. Her hat flew off during the hat race, and by the time she jumped down, picked it up, and scrambled back on Captain, she was completely out of the running. Then, during the Sandsurfing, Luke fell off the board when Carly rounded the first corner and their team was disqualified. The other events passed in a blur, with Carly finishing fourth in the pole bending and third in the obstacle course.

At long last, it was time for the barrel race. Carly played with her leather reins and fidgeted in the saddle as she waited her turn. Finally, the announcement came. "Luke Carsten, next rider. Carly McCallister, on deck, Ross Buchanon, in the hole."

Carly took a deep breath as she watched Luke trot Sunny into the corral. She had never been so nervous. She was sure everyone knew exactly what she was going to do. She glanced at the riders around her. No one was even looking at her. All eyes were fixed on Luke and his mare.

Carly watched, too, as they turned the third barrel and raced for home. Their run was perfect. "18.8 seconds, folks!" Mrs. Hays shouted. "Luke has just moved himself into first place."

For a minute, Carly was tempted to forget her plan. With only three riders left to run in the race, it was a pretty safe bet that no one else had a chance of beating Luke. And Carly had already lost every other contest here. Maybe that was enough.

Then her dream of Savannah Winters riding

Captain floated through her mind. She shook her head to clear the image. There was no other way. If she wanted to keep Captain, she had to lose this race.

Luke was leaving the ring as Carly entered it. "Great job. You finally broke into the 18s!"

"Thanks," Luke said. Then he trotted out of the arena, calling "good luck" to Carly over his shoulder.

"Thanks," Carly echoed.

She scanned the sidelines. Mom and Dad stood just outside the ring, even with the second barrel.

Mom waved. "You can do it," she called.

Carly waved back, but she couldn't force herself to smile. She turned Captain away from her parents, dug in her spurs, and raced towards the first barrel.

Carly knew she had to make it look as if she was doing her best. She guided Captain into a tight turn, then headed toward the next barrel.

When they reached it, Carly pulled Captain up sharply and turned a fraction too soon. She could feel Captain fight the steel bit in his mouth as she deliberately guided his shoulder into the barrel. Carly heard the crowd moan and she knew they had good reason. Dust flew up around them as the barrel tumbled over.

Carly ignored it. Her mission accomplished, she directed Captain toward the third barrel. She guided him into a perfect turn and they flew home. She knew the five-second penalty she'd earned because of the tipped barrel would take them completely out of the winner's bracket. She didn't even slow Captain down when they reached the gate. They charged past the startled gate holder and through the opening, scattering horses and riders as they went.

"Carly, wait up." She heard Luke call to her but she ignored him.

She galloped Captain past the bleachers and through the open field until they came to the road. There, at last, she pulled Captain to a halt and glanced behind her. Luke was nowhere in sight.

Carly and Captain were still there when she heard Mrs. Hays give the results of the race over the loudspeaker. First place went to Luke and second place to a girl from Hartington. Carly's name wasn't mentioned at all. She buried her face in Captain's mane and burst into tears.

Chapter 9
Jewel and Captain

Carly sat cross-legged on her bed, surrounded by photographs.

"May I come in?" Mom called from the other side of the door.

"Just a minute." Carly backhanded her tears from her face and stuffed the pictures into the shoebox.

"Okay. Come in." She sat up as Mom walked into the room.

"Hi, Honey. How are you feeling?"

"Fine," Carly said.

Mom reached out and wiped a tear from Carly's cheek. "Carly, I know you're upset about your performance today. But everyone has a bad day now and then. You know that."

"I know," Carly said. "I'm not crying about that." And she wasn't. Not really. After all, she planned to lose those races at the Play Day. So she couldn't be sad about it. And yet, part of her knew that was exactly why she was crying.

Carly reached for a tissue and blew her nose. "I've been looking at some old pictures of Captain and thinking about all the good times we've had." Carly pushed the box across the bed.

Mom reached into the box and pulled out a handful of photographs. She sat down on the edge of the bed and shuffled through them.

"Oh, Carly. Here's a picture of you and Captain when you won your first barrel race." She looked through a few more, then paused again. "And here you are with Luke at the fair. Was this just last year? You two are the same size in this picture. Now he's as tall as his mother."

"I know." Carly leaned over Mom's shoulder to look at it.

"Look. A picture of Captain and his mama, Jewel. This must have been taken right after your grandpa bought them." Mom sighed. "Do you know Jewel was the only horse I've ever been brave enough to ride?"

Carly looked at Mom in surprise. "You used to ride? I didn't know that."

"Well, I obviously wasn't in the same league as you and Luke. In fact, you probably wouldn't even consider it riding. I don't think we ever went faster than a trot, and we never left the corral. Not even once!" Mom smiled at the memory. "When I was growing up, your grandpa always wanted me to become a rider. He so loved having horses when he was a kid and he thought everyone should learn to ride."

Her voice dropped. "But horses just scared me. I didn't want anything to do with them. And finally, he gave up trying. Until I married your father, that is."

"What do you mean? What happened after you married Dad?"

"I moved to the country, of course. Your grandpa loved it here. He and Grandma used to drive out from Lincoln every chance they got. Especially after you were born!"

Mom stared at the picture in her hand, but Carly could tell she wasn't actually seeing it. "When I first came to the farm, everything was so strange. After growing up in Lincoln, I didn't know the first thing about being a country girl. And your dad was always so busy, he didn't have time to teach me." She paused, absently rubbing the sides of her forehead with her fingertips, as if trying to recall the exact details. Carly held her breath and didn't say anything. She didn't want her mom to stop.

"Your grandpa could tell something was wrong. And in his own way, he tried to help. Of course, with Grandpa, helping really means getting what he always wanted in the first place," she said, smiling. "One day, he showed up at the farm with this rust-colored mare and her baby colt. 'I know what you're thinking, Caroline,' he said, 'but this colt is a present for Carly. And I couldn't very well have brought him here without his mama, could I?'"

Mom stopped and shifted on the bed. "He was right, as usual. Bringing Jewel to the farm was just what I needed. There we were, two first-time mommas, trying to figure out how to raise our babies. I used to talk to her for hours. Some days I felt like she was the only friend I had." Carefully, she traced the outline of the horse in the picture. "She was such a beautiful mare. I cried for three days when she died."

"Oh, Mom, I'm sorry," Carly whispered. "I didn't know."

"I know you didn't, Honey, but that's okay," Mom said softly. "You were only six at the time and so in love with that baby colt of hers." She wiped the tears from her own eyes and gave Carly a hug. Then she set the stack of photographs back in their box.

"Well, enough of this," she said. "I came in to cheer you up, and all I've done is tell sad stories that make us both cry." She walked to the door, then looked back at Carly. "I came in to tell you that everything is going to work out for the best. But the truth is, I can't promise you that, and neither can your dad. Saying good-bye to someone, or something, you love is never easy. But sometimes, you don't have any other choice."

"I've raised Captain from a colt. I love him. How can I leave him when we move to Lincoln?" Carly asked, grabbing her pillow and hugging it against her stomach.

Mom paused in the doorway and looked at her. "Carlene Louise, Captain was meant to live in the country. If you love him, how could you want him to be any place else?" With that, she slipped out, closing the door behind her.

Chapter 10
Hiding Out

Carly tucked the letter into her back pocket and sprinted across the yard toward the corral. As she ran, she scanned the farmyard for Mom or Dad. They were nowhere in sight. She breathed a sigh of relief, crawled over the wooden fence, and headed for Captain. He stood in the shade of the barn, swishing flies with his tail. "Howdy, Cap," she whispered. "You ready for a ride?"

It had been six weeks since the Play Day. Six weeks, six more horse shows, and six more afternoons of losing every event she and Captain entered. And with each passing day, it got harder and harder to face her parents or Luke. She was sure someone would start to ask questions that she didn't want to answer.

Questions like "Why are you having so much trouble with that second barrel?" Or, "How many poles did you knock down at practice tonight?" Or, "Why does Captain seem to fight you every time you enter the ring?" Questions Carly couldn't answer, not without making up a lie. So Carly spent her time looking for ways to avoid talking to them altogether.

Actually, it wasn't that hard to do. Dad was busy getting their place ready for the auction. Mom was always on the road between their farm and Lincoln. And now that it was summer, Luke was busy helping his dad in the hayfields or with the summer guests staying at the Castle. None of them had time to pay any attention to what Carly was doing.

Carly saddled Captain as quickly as she could. She climbed on his back and Captain danced and shook his head, eager to be off.

"Whoa, Cap. Easy does it," Carly said. She pulled gently on the reins and turned Captain toward the road. If her parents or Luke did catch sight of her, Carly knew they would think she was headed for their back pasture to practice. After all, she should be. Tomorrow was the Fourth of July. She and Captain were supposed to race at the Nebraska Centennial

Celebration and Rodeo in St. Claire.

But as soon as Carly turned the corner and knew she was safely out of sight, she headed for the creek. She held Captain to a walk until they were clear of the trees that sheltered their lane. Then, with a gentle kick, she urged the big sorrel into a canter. Captain took off, building up speed with every stride. Soon, the hay bales and the wooden fence posts blended into gold and brown and green swirls as Carly raced past them. The wind cooled her face and the pounding of Captain's hooves matched the pounding of her heart. This is what she loved most about riding—this race with the wind. How could she give this up? Why did she have to? It wasn't fair. She wouldn't do it!

When a sheen of sweat appeared on Captain's neck and his breathing became labored, Carly knew it was time to slow down. She tugged on the reins, but Captain fought the command to stop. It seemed he wanted to race the wind forever. Carly understood. She thought how wonderful it would be if they could keep going and going and going until they had run away from all their problems.

But that wasn't going to happen. And Captain needed to slow down, now, or he would overheat.

Carly pulled on the reins with more force. This time, Captain obeyed. His strides grew shorter as he slowed his pace to a canter.

By the time they had reached the creek, he was trotting and his breathing had returned to normal. "Now that's what I call a ride," Carly said. "I think you deserve to rest before we go back." Captain nickered and nodded his head.

Carly dismounted and led him to the creek. Resting her arms on the seat of the saddle, Carly waited for Captain to drink his fill from the cool, clear water. Then she tied his reins to a nearby tree and left him to graze on the sweet prairie grass.

Carly wandered back to the creek and sat down on the bank. She took off her boots and socks and sank her feet into the water, watching the ripples around her ankles spread out, then disappear.

She loved it here. This was the place she escaped to when she needed a quiet place to think. It was also the place she fled to whenever she was sad or lonely.

For the past six weeks, it seemed like that was all the time. Six weeks of helping her parents sort through their most prized possessions, deciding what they would keep and what they would sell at the auction.

Six weeks of long solitary rides, saying goodbye to the places she loved most. Six weeks of deliberately tipping barrels and poles. Six weeks of deliberately losing.

Carly had never given much thought to losing before this summer. But ever since that first horse show, she had thought about it a lot. She and Captain had been winning at rodeos and horse shows in this part of the state for the past two years. They had always been known as the team to beat. Now that wasn't true. Luke and Sunny had that role, and Carly and Captain were just another horse and rider.

Carly hated that idea, just like she hated losing. She wanted to beat Luke and prove to everyone that she and Captain were still the best team around.

She pulled the letter from Grandma out of her back pocket and opened it one more time. Grandma had been happy to put a newspaper ad in the Lincoln paper as a gift for Carly's birthday. She even agreed to keep it a secret from Carly's folks. "They have enough to worry about now," Grandma said.

When Carly saw the letter in the mailbox this morning, she snatched it out and tore it open. She was sure it would be good news. But it wasn't. Not one person had answered the ad.

Carly picked up a flat stone and pitched it toward the creek. She watched as it skipped four times before sinking. She felt just like that rock. No matter how hard she fought to stay afloat, eventually she was going to sink.

"No!" she shouted, scaring a rabbit from its hiding spot. "I am not a stone to be tossed away. I will not lose Captain." She grabbed her socks and boots, pulled them on, and tramped back to where Captain was grazing, undisturbed by her burst of anger.

"Everyone who is anyone will be at the rodeo tomorrow," she said, draping her arms around Captain's neck. She buried her face in his soft warm coat, trying not to cry. "If we win, Mr. Winters will know you're still the best barrel-racing horse around. And then there'll be no way to keep him from buying you."

She untied the reins from the tree and pulled herself into the saddle. "There's nothing else to do," she said. "As much as I hate it, we just have to keep losing." She turned Captain away from the creek and galloped up the gravel road toward home.

Chapter 11
Caught

Carly turned Captain into their lane and trotted for the barn. Dad sat perched on the top rail of their corral.

"How was practice?" he asked.

"Fine," Carly replied. She dismounted and wrapped the reins around a post. Then she threw the stirrup over the saddle horn and unhooked the cinch strap.

Dad jumped down from the fence. "What about that second barrel? Are you still having trouble with it?"

"A little," she admitted. "I'm not sure what the problem is. Captain just can't seem to get the timing right." Carly kept her eyes glued to the leather strap in front of her while she talked. She knew she couldn't look at Dad and lie to him at the same time.

"I don't know," he said. "It seems to me you're the one with the problem. I think you're spending too much time worrying about the move, instead of concentrating on the races."

"Well, of course I'm worried!" Carly cried. She turned and looked at Dad. "This is my home. This is where all my friends are. I don't want to move to Lincoln. I don't want to go to school there. And I sure don't want to sell Captain to Savannah Winters!"

Carly grabbed the horn of the saddle, pulled it and the pad from Captain's back, and let them drop to the ground. Dust flew everywhere. Captain snorted and tried to pull away, but the tethered reins held him tight.

"Whoa," Carly said. She grabbed the reins and patted the big horse's neck at the same time. She was ashamed of her outburst. It wasn't Captain's fault they were moving.

She waited for the reprimand that was sure to come from Dad, but nothing happened. Finally, Carly got up the courage to turn around. Dad was leaning against the corral. The bill of his cap shadowed his face, and Carly couldn't tell if his eyes were opened or closed.

Carly stared at him, not sure what to do. Finally, Dad spoke. "It's my home, too, Carly," he said, in a voice so soft she almost didn't catch the words. "I've loved this place since the first time I set eyes on it. I love the smell of the pine trees in the lane. I love the purple of the alfalfa fields when they're in full bloom. Most of all, I love to lie in bed at night and listen to the sound of the crickets and the coyotes and the barn owls talking to each other and singing me to sleep."

Carly wanted to break in, but she didn't know how. She cleared her throat, but Dad didn't seem to notice. He just kept talking, almost like Carly wasn't there. "I asked your mom to marry me, right over there, under the big oak tree. The day you were born, I planted the apple tree in the backyard. And when you were three, I helped you catch your first fish, down at the creek." He paused and looked straight at her. His eyes were wet and shining.

Carly wondered if Dad was going to cry. The thought made her sick to her stomach. She had never seen Dad cry before. She didn't want to see it now.

"The truth is, Carly, I've got so many memories tied up here, in this place, I hurt just at the thought of moving."

"Then why, Dad? Why do we have to leave?" Carly asked.

"Because, Carly, it's time. For fifteen years I've been asking your mom to give country living a chance. I was sure that with a little time, she would come to love it as much as I do." He laughed, but it was the saddest sound Carly had ever heard. "I was wrong. All the time in the world isn't going to make one bit of difference. And as much as I love this old place, I love your mom more."

"You're wrong, Dad. Mom loves it here!"

"Carly, you know that's not true. Your mom tolerates this place, but she doesn't love it. Now, with Grandpa so sick and your mom driving back and forth to Lincoln all the time, this place is just one more thing she has to worry about."

He sighed, then waved his arms in all directions. "Just open your eyes and look around you. The barn and house are both in need of a fresh coat of paint, and the shed is filled with rusty old tools and machinery parts that are of no use to anyone anymore. We get our water from a well and our clothes from a second-hand store. Your mom deserves better than this. And I can give it to her. But only if we sell the farm and move to Lincoln."

"Dad, please don't make us move. Please."

"I've been thinking about this for a long time now." Dad paused to clear his throat. "It's time to stop fighting and accept what's happening. For your mom's sake, and for mine."

"I'm trying Dad. But it's so hard," Carly whispered. She slipped her arms around Captain's neck and wrapped her fingers in the golden strands of his mane. "Maybe if . . . isn't there some way we can keep Captain?"

"We've been through this before. I've already agreed to sell him to Mr. Winters. I won't go back on my word."

"But what if Mr. Winters decides he doesn't want to buy him?" Carly asked.

"I've already told you. Mr. Winters is not going to change his mind about the sale."

"Not even if we keep losing races? I thought you said he only wanted the best for Savannah. The way Captain keeps clipping those poles and barrels—" Carly knew as soon as the words were out that she'd made a mistake. The look on her father's face confirmed it.

"Just a minute," he said. "Are you telling me you've

been tipping those things on purpose? That you've been trying to lose?"

Carly wanted to deny it, but she knew it wouldn't do any good. She had pretty much admitted it already. She tightened her arms around Captain's neck and took a deep breath.

"I had to, Dad," she said. "It was the only way I could think of to stop you from selling Captain." She looked up at him. "And I have to stop you, Dad. Because I'm not leaving Riley without him."

"Carlene Louise, you have no choice. And the sooner you face up to it, the better." Dad rested his hand on Carly's shoulder and gave it a squeeze. "Now, you get that horse put away and run on up to the house for supper. I want to leave bright and early for the rodeo tomorrow."

Dad picked up the saddle and pad from the ground and headed to the barn. At the door he turned back to Carly. "And there will be no more foolishness going on in that ring. Tomorrow, I expect to see you and Captain win those races."

Chapter 12
Good Luck, Bad Luck

"Carly, wait up!"

Carly stopped. She stared across the damp, muddy field toward the row of parked cars, trucks, and horse trailers, searching for Luke. He appeared between two trailers and sprinted toward her, dodging puddles.

"I've been looking all over for you," he said. "Do you want to hide out in our pickup until the rain stops? We can share my thermos of cocoa."

"Great," Carly said. "That sounds better than the cold pop we have in our cooler."

"Drinking hot chocolate on the Fourth of July!" Luke said. "Who would have guessed it?"

"Grandpa," Carly said, with a little smile. "He always said if you don't like the weather in Nebraska, you just have to wait an hour. It'll change."

Carly and Luke slipped and slid their way across the field, laughing and talking as their boots sank into the wet, spongy grass with each step they took.

As soon as they reached the truck, they scrambled into the front seat of the cab. Carly peeled off her rain poncho and kicked it to the floor. Luke grabbed a green thermos and two cups from behind the seat. He filled one of the cups with cocoa and handed it to Carly.

Carly took a sip and savored the sweet taste of chocolate on her tongue before letting it slide down her throat. Then she looked over at Luke. "You said you were looking for me. How come?"

"No special reason. I just wanted to wish you good luck."

"Oh." Carly bit her bottom lip and stared out the window at the wet grass. "Thanks. I guess you think I'll be needing it, the way I've been riding lately."

"I didn't mean it that way. It's just that, well . . . it's mighty slick out there, and—"

"And since I haven't won one race all summer, even in the best of weather, I sure don't have much chance of pulling it off today."

"Carly, that's not what I'm saying. I know how much time you spend each day practicing. No one is more dedicated than you."

Carly stared at Luke. What was that supposed to mean? Was he trying to be funny? Did he know she'd been losing the races on purpose? No. He couldn't know that. No one knew that except Dad. Suddenly, Carly realized Luke was still talking.

"You're just having some bad luck, that's all," he was saying. "It could happen to anyone. Especially with everything going on this summer. It doesn't mean . . . ."

Luke stopped himself, but Carly figured she knew what was coming next, anyway.

"It doesn't mean what? That I can't win? That I'm not quite as good as I thought I was?" Carly didn't look at Luke when she spoke. Instead, she kept her eyes on the droplets of rain that chased each other down the window.

"No, of course not. I think you and Captain are the best. It's just that you're trying too hard. You need to relax and let Captain do his job. He could run those patterns blindfolded. Just give him his head and let him do it."

Carly couldn't believe her ears. Luke was serious. He really didn't know she'd been skipping practices and losing on purpose. Instead, he thought she was doing her best to win, but it wasn't enough. Dad was right. It was time to forget her plan and go back to winning.

The plan wasn't working the way she thought, anyway. Luke didn't believe for a minute that Captain was to blame for their sudden losing streak. And if Luke didn't believe it, Carly knew that no one else believed it either.

"You're right," Carly said, pounding her fist on the dashboard. "I'm tired of losing." She opened the passenger door. "Come on, Luke. Let's go. Rain or no rain, I'm going to win everything today. You just wait and see!"

Two hours later, the sun came out and the horse show started again. Carly no longer felt cold and wet. Now, she was just hot and sticky and anxious to have the barrel race over. She nervously flicked the reins back and forth while she waited and watched nineteen other barrel racers, including Luke, run the pattern before her. In fact, despite the wet and muddy field, Luke and Sunny's pattern was almost perfect. When their race was over, they were first in the standings.

"And our last rider in this division, Carly McCallister."

"Finally!" Carly muttered. "I was beginning to think they'd forgotten us."

"Good luck," Luke called as she passed him. "You can do it. Give Captain his head and let him run."

Carly gritted her teeth. She knew how to run a barrel pattern. She didn't need Luke, or anyone else, telling her what to do. She nodded at him, then headed for the ring.

She pulled Captain to a stop inside the arena and waited for the judge's signal. He nodded. Taking one last deep breath, Carly dug her heels into Captain's sides and galloped towards the first barrel.

Carly breathed a sigh of relief when she and Captain raced by the second barrel without touching it. She imagined Dad was doing the same. But the weeks of lost races and skipped practices had taken their toll. Carly knew she had wasted too much time circling the first two barrels. If she was going to beat Luke, she would have to make up for that lost time. "Come on, Captain, faster," she shouted, as they closed in on the final barrel.

Carly was so intent on pushing Captain she didn't see the slick patch surrounding the barrel until they were on top of it. She tried to slow Captain down and guide him away from it, but it was too late. She felt Captain's legs go out from under him as he began to slide. Horse and rider fought to keep their balance, but it was no use. Captain's left front leg buckled and he went down, head first. Carly kicked her feet out of the stirrups and pushed off the saddle. Ducking her head as she hit the ground, she rolled until she was safely out of range of Captain's flailing hooves.

With Carly off his back, Captain regained his footing and trotted slowly toward the front gate. Carly picked herself up, snatched her straw hat from out of the mud, and headed for the gate as well. She grabbed Captain's reins and led him out of the arena.

Mom and Dad met her outside the gate. "Carly, are you okay?" Mom asked. She pulled her into a crushing embrace, despite the fact Carly was covered in mud from head to toe. "You nearly scared me half to death."

"I'm fine." She pushed herself out of Mom's arms and looked over at Dad. "But I can't say the same for Captain. He's limping."

Dad ran his hands firmly down Captain's left front

leg. Captain whinnied sharply and tried to pull away. "Carly," he said, "I don't like the looks of this. Go find Doc Baker and tell him to get over here as soon as possible. I think Captain may have fractured his knee."

Chapter 13
Moving Grandma

"Carlene Louise, where are you? We should have left fifteen minutes ago."

It had been more than a week since Captain's fall at the Fourth of July Celebration. After the veterinarian, Doc Baker, finished examining Captain's leg that day, he announced there was no need for alarm. Captain's knee wasn't fractured; it was just a bad sprain. Doc suggested complete rest for two weeks and no more competition for the rest of the summer. By next season, he said, Captain's leg would be as good as new.

No need for alarm? Was he crazy? To Carly's way of thinking, there was every need. She had wasted the first part of their summer losing races. Now, because of one little patch of mud, their entire rodeo season was over. For all she knew, this would be her last year ever to barrel race and pole bend and she was going out a loser.

Then, to make matters worse, since she couldn't ride for two weeks anyway, her parents decided she could use that time to help Mom and Grandma in Lincoln. This week, they were going to rearrange bedrooms. Grandma was moving into a room downstairs. Then Mom and Dad would have Grandpa and Grandma's bedroom, and Carly would move into the room her mom had when she was a girl.

"Carly! I'm waiting!" Mom called. "What are you doing?"

"I'm coming. I just need to put on my shoes." Carly got down on her hands and knees and peered under the bed. She knew her tennis shoes were there somewhere.

Finally, she found them, hidden behind her box of pictures. She pushed the box aside, fished out her shoes and slipped them on.

Not bothering to tie them, she jogged down the stairs and into the kitchen. It was empty. Mom must already be in the car. Carly grabbed a couple of chocolate chip cookies, then pushed the back door open and headed outside.

"Want one?" she asked as she crawled into the front seat of the car.

"Cookies? We just finished breakfast! Don't you ever get full?"

Carly shrugged.

"What took you so long?" Mom asked, as she headed down the gravel road toward the highway. "Grandma is going to wonder what's become of us."

"My shoes," Carly said, pointing to her feet. "I couldn't find them."

"I see. Well, tie them, please. You know I don't like to see you running around with the laces dragging in the dirt."

As Carly knotted the weathered ties, she thought about the work ahead of them. Today they were going to move Grandma's bed into Grandpa's office. They all knew Grandpa would never use it again. Of course, nobody said that. Instead, they talked about Grandma and how this move downstairs would be easier for her.

Carly wondered if Grandpa knew he was losing his office, forever. Sometimes she felt like she and Grandpa were in the same situation. Life was happening all around them but they weren't part of it.

People were making decisions that would change their lives forever, and they couldn't do a thing about it. They were trapped. Prisoners.

"Mom, will we see Grandpa today?" Carly asked.

"I think so," Mom said. "Grandma said he's feeling much better."

They had tried to visit him last week when they were in Lincoln, but he was sleeping, so they just left a box of chocolates on his nightstand. Then, the next day, Grandma said he didn't feel up to having company. Later, Carly overheard Grandma say the chocolates had given him diarrhea and he was too embarrassed to see them.

Thinking about Grandpa made her sad. She dug out her library book, *The Mouse and the Motorcycle*, from under the front seat. Maybe getting lost in Keith and Ralph's world would help Carly forget everything that was going on in her life.

It worked. Almost before Carly knew it, they were pulling into Grandma's driveway. Grandma was sitting on the front porch, reading the paper. She waved but did not get up.

"Oh, dear," Mom said. "Your grandmother is sitting, and it isn't even eleven o'clock. Her back must be acting up again. Carly, you carry in those empty boxes from the backseat. Take them right upstairs to her room. I'll unload the stuff from the trunk."

Carly grabbed the boxes and headed toward the house. "Hi, Grandma," she said, as she bounded up the steps to the porch. "How are you?"

"Never better," Grandma said, with a smile. "It was such a nice day, I decided to wait for you here in the sunshine."

"Good. Mom was afraid your back was hurting."

"That mom of yours," said Grandma, winking. "She always was nothing but a worrywart."

"I heard that!" Carly's mom called from the driveway.

"Oops!" Grandma said, and Carly grinned.

Then Carly leaned in and whispered, "Any calls about the ad?"

"No, Dear. Not even one. But don't give up hope. I'm going to call the newspaper and have them run it again next week."

"Thanks for trying, Grandma."

"What are you two troublemakers whispering about?" Mom asked, coming up behind them.

"Nothing important," Carly said. She kissed

Grandma on the cheek, then brushed past and headed inside with her load of boxes. After she had carried the boxes up the stairs and set them down at the foot of Grandma's bed, she headed down the hallway to her mom's old room.

Flopping down on the bed, Carly rested her chin on her folded arms and closed her eyes. It didn't make any difference. She could still see the room, just the way it was. A white bedspread with pink and blue flowers covered the huge four-poster bed. A bulletin board hung on the wall beside the bed, plastered with photographs of Mom as a kid. A bookcase beside the bed was filled with old dolls and stuffed animals and some of her mom's favorite books, like *Mr. Popper's Penguins*, *Homer Price*, and *The Hundred Dresses*. On the wall across from it was a framed coin collection of pennies, nickels, and dimes, some of them forty and fifty years old.

Carly reached up and plucked a picture from the board. The girl in the photograph looked like she was on her way to some grand adventure and had just paused long enough for the picture to be snapped before she took off running again.

Carly tried to imagine Mom as that little girl, but

she just couldn't. Mom never smiled this way, with her eyes sparkling and her tongue peeking out from between her teeth.

Carly traced the girl's smile. It was weird how time could change people, forever. Carly wondered how this move to Lincoln would change her. Would she ever ride again? Would her own daughter stare at a picture of her twenty years from now and wonder who that person was and what had happened to her?

"Time for lunch," Mom called. "Come on down. We'll get started working after we eat."

Carly rolled off the bed. Soon, all of the stuffed animals and dolls and coins would be gone from this room. Carly's show ribbons would take the place of the coin collection and her box of pictures would be tucked safely under the bed.

But Carly knew this room would never really be hers, no matter how long they lived in this house. Her room would always be a room with blue walls and a wooden floor in a farmhouse three hours from here. And this room would always belong to a little girl with sparkling eyes and a laughing smile who looked for grand adventures around each corner.

Chapter 14
Good News, Bad News

"Jasper. Are you sure? Doc Baker says that Captain's leg is going to be fine. It was just a bad sprain. Carly's already riding him again. By next season, he'll be good as new."

Carly stood inside the corral, brushing Captain's mane while she listened to Dad and Mr. Winters talk. It had been three weeks since Captain's fall and, like Dad said, his leg seemed to be healing just fine.

"I don't care what Doc Baker says," Mr. Winters protested. "That leg is always going to give that horse problems. I saw him go down with your girl. I won't take the chance of him doing the same with Savannah."

"Jasper, I understand how you feel. My heart

stopped when I saw Captain slip and go down. But it was just an accident. It would never happen again."

"I'm sorry, Ray. I know you think I'm overreacting. But I've already wasted my money buying one problem horse for Savannah. And from what I've seen this summer, it looks like Captain is just as unpredictable and dangerous as Buttercup's Princess."

"Unpredictable? Dangerous? That's ridiculous. You won't find a more disciplined horse anywhere!"

Carly stopped brushing Captain's coat and stared at Dad. He never got angry. But Carly could tell he was angry now.

"I think you're making a mistake, Jasper," Dad said. "But if that's the way you feel, I won't try and change your mind. It was nice of you to drive out to tell us, rather than just calling on the phone." Carly watched as Dad opened the door of Mr. Winters' pickup.

"I'm sorry, Ray. If he really is as well-trained as you say, you'll have no trouble selling him to someone else." With that, Mr. Winters slid into his pickup, slammed the door and drove away, leaving a cloud of dust behind him.

As Carly watched the truck disappear around the bend, she felt a bubble of excitement build up inside her. She needed to tell someone, and fast. Grandma. Luke. Someone!

Dad walked to the corral and climbed up on the top rail to sit. "You heard?" he asked.

"Yeah," Carly replied, grinning. "Mr. Winters doesn't want to buy Captain after all."

"That's right. He thinks Captain's too dangerous for Savannah. Too dangerous! Can you believe it?" He slammed his fist down on the rail.

The bubble inside burst. "What's going to happen now, Dad?" she asked.

"I don't know, Carly. I guess we'll have to sell him at our auction next week."

"At the auction?" Carly stared at Dad. "We can't do that. What if someone mean buys him? Someone who's never had a horse and doesn't know the first thing about how to care for him? Why, he could even end up at some dog food factory!" Carly felt her stomach muscles tighten. She was sure she was going to be sick.

"Now, Carly, don't start talking nonsense. There are lots of good people in this part of the country who know Captain and his reputation. Like Mr. Winters said, we'll have no trouble finding a home for him."

"But if he's sold at the auction, he could end up anywhere. South Dakota or Iowa or Missouri." Carly kicked at a dirt clod, sending it flying. "At least when Mr. Winters was buying him, I knew where he was going to be."

"I'm sorry, Carly. And I know exactly how you feel. That's the main reason I worked so hard to convince Mr. Winters to buy him in the first place. But now, I don't know what else to do. Time is running out. Two weeks from today we'll be leaving for Lincoln. And like your mom and I've told you all summer long, there's no way we can afford to take Captain with us."

Dad jumped down from the fence. "I'd better go tell your mom the news. The way Mr. Winters was hightailing it out of here, everybody in the county will know what's happened before nightfall. And the last thing we need is for your mom to hear the news from someone else before she hears it from us."

Carly watched Dad climb the hill toward their house. Then she turned back to Captain. "Well, I got my wish," she said, rubbing the white diamond on Captain's forehead. "Mr. Winters isn't going to buy you after all."

She gave Captain a hug and returned the brush and

curry comb to the barn. Then she followed Dad up the hill to their house. As she dragged her boots through the dirt, she imagined she could hear Grandpa's voice, whispering to her. *Be careful what you wish for, Girl. You never know how those wishes will come true.*

Chapter 15
A Morning Ride

Carly woke up early the next morning. A woodpecker was rapping a tuneless song on the oak tree outside her window. She could hear Angel barking at the woodpecker and the rooster crowing in the hen house.

Carly dressed quietly. She tiptoed down the hall, taking care not to wake Mom and Dad. She grabbed the camera from the top of the refrigerator, her jacket from the coat rack on the back porch, and headed out the door.

With the camera dangling from her wrist, Carly jogged down the path to the corral. She slipped the bridle over Captain's head but didn't bother to saddle him. Instead, she tipped over a five-gallon feed bucket, used it as a stool, and hopped up on Captain's back.

As Captain trotted down the lane, Carly thought about the future. The auction was only one week away now. In less than two weeks, she would actually be living in Lincoln, Nebraska.

For the first time, Carly tried to imagine what it would be like to live in a city. What sounds would wake her there? How would she spend her early morning and late afternoon hours, if she didn't have chores to do, a horse to ride, and a creek to go fishing in whenever she wanted?

What was school like in the city? How many kids would she have in her class? At Carsten Castle, there were only nine kids, kindergarten through the sixth grade, and Luke was the only other person in her class. What if she was way behind in math or reading or social studies? What if she got lost traveling from one class to the next? What if none of the kids in Lincoln liked her or wanted to be her friend?

The questions surprised and scared her. She had spent so much time this summer worrying about Captain, she had managed to avoid thoughts about the changes this move would bring to her life.

She aimed the camera toward the lane to get a shot of the house and the trees surrounding it. Then she clasped the camera tightly in her left fist and urged Captain into a canter. When they reached the road, she headed west, toward Luke's place.

"Captain, I know Dad's right. I can't stop us from moving to Lincoln. But what am I going to do about you?" she asked. "I won't let you be sold at the auction, like a piece of furniture or some old manure spreader."

Suddenly, the quiet morning air was broken by the sound of a horse's sharp whinny. Captain threw back his head and gave an answering call. Luke's buckskin mare raced over the hill, pulling up sharply when she reached the barbed wire fence that separated the Carsten's pasture from the county road.

"Morning, Sunny," Carly called. "May I take your picture, please?"

Sunny nickered and tossed her head, as if to say "yes." Then she reached her neck across the fence. Carly snapped a picture of Captain and Sunny nudging noses.

"Captain," she said, "I think you're going to miss Sunny more than you're going to miss me." While Carly took aim with the camera, over the hill came a small brown Shetland pony. He trotted up next to Sunny, his sides heaving as he fought for every breath.

"There you are, Flash. I wondered where you were hiding." Carly smiled fondly at the old horse. Pulling a sugar cube out of her jacket pocket, she offered it to him. "I hear you're getting too old to leave the pasture. Poor Josie. Just when she needs a horse of her own."

That's when it hit her. Luke had been right. The Carstens were the perfect family for Captain. "Come on," she said, tugging on the big sorrel's reins and turning him around. "We've got to get home. Now!"

Chapter 16
One Final Plan

"Hi, Luke. You busy?" Carly asked. She shifted the telephone to her left ear and settled on the floor of the kitchen, resting her back against the wall.

"Naw. What's up?"

"Mr. Winters came out to see Dad yesterday. He's not buying Captain after all. He's sure Captain's never going to be the same again, after our fall."

"Carly, that's great!"

"No, it isn't," Carly said. "It's terrible. Because now Dad says we have to sell Captain at our farm sale. He could end up a million miles away from here."

"Gee, I didn't think about that. I'm really sorry, Carly."

"Don't be, because we're not going to let that happen."

"We're not?"

"No, we're not."

"And how are we going to stop it?"

Carly could hear the suspicion in Luke's voice. She imagined the look on his face and smiled. "We're going to get someone else to buy Captain. Someone who'll take care of him and love him as much as I do."

"Carly, are you crazy? Where are we going to find someone to buy Captain?"

"I already found someone. Your folks."

"My folks? Why would they want to buy Captain?"

"For Josie! It was your idea in the first place, remember? You said that Captain would be the perfect horse for her."

"Carly, I was just kidding."

"No you weren't. And even if you were, it's true. He's gentle and he's an expert in the ring. You said he could run the pattern blindfolded if he had to. All Josie has to do is hold on, and Captain will do the rest. He's the perfect horse for her to take in 4-H."

"I don't know," Luke said. "I don't think this idea is going to work. After all, Josie won't be able to take a horse in 4-H for at least two more years."

Carly could just picture him, frowning and shaking

his head as he talked.

"Plus, Captain is almost seventeen hands tall! I think my mom is planning to buy her another small horse, like Flash. And even if they wanted to buy Captain, there's no way my dad can afford to pay the kind of money that Mr. Winters was going to pay for him."

"Why do you always do this? This idea will work. I know it will!" Carly pounded her fist on the floor in frustration. "First of all, your folks would be silly to pass up a good opportunity to buy a horse if one dropped into their laps. Secondly, even if Captain is a lot bigger than Flash, Josie's ridden him lots of times, and she's never had one bit of trouble. Last, and most important, if Dad sells Captain at the auction, there's no telling how much we'll get for him. Your dad and my dad both know that. So I figure, if your dad makes a reasonable offer, my dad will jump at it, even if it's not as much as he was hoping for."

"I guess, if you look at it like that, it does sort of make sense," Luke said. "Of course, I'm not the one you have to convince."

"I know that. But would you at least talk to your folks about it? Please?"

"Okay," Luke agreed. "I'll talk to them. But I can't promise it'll do any good."

Carly glanced at the clock on the wall. "Look, Luke, I've got to get started on chores. Thanks a bunch. Let me know as soon as you've had a chance to talk to your mom and dad."

Carly hung up the phone. She sat quietly for a few seconds, tracing the pattern on the worn kitchen linoleum with her fist. Then she pushed herself up and headed for the door.

Chapter 17
The Letter

Carly pulled a long blade of grass from the side of the road to chew on as she walked to the mailbox. Angel raced ahead, sniffing for rabbits in the ditch, but Carly paid no attention. There were only four days left now before their farm auction, and she hadn't heard a word from either Luke or her grandma. Everything she had tried so far had failed. She couldn't give up. But she didn't know what else to do. She was running out of time.

Carly took a deep breath and pulled open the door of the box. Inside, there was a large package from the auctioneer in charge of their sale, a catalog from Montgomery Ward, and a pink envelope, addressed to her, from Grandma.

Carly tore the envelope open and scanned the letter inside. She couldn't believe it! Grandma had finally gotten a response to their ad. A stable five miles outside of Lincoln was willing to board Captain for free if Carly agreed to work ten hours a week for them. Carly collapsed on the side of the road and Angel jumped on top of her. She laughed out loud and read the letter again. It was true! She could take Captain with her to Lincoln. All her troubles were over! Wait until she told Mom and Dad!

Oh, yeah, Mom and Dad. Okay, so maybe all of her troubles weren't over, yet. But almost. All she had to do was tell them Grandma had found a home for Captain as a gift for her. She didn't have to say it was her idea, did she? And even if it was her idea, did that really matter? All that really mattered was that Captain would not have to be sold at the auction.

Carly jumped up and took off running. "Come on, Angel. We have lots to do!"

Carly found her mom in the living room, packing. "Look, Mom," she shouted, waving the letter. "It's just like you said! Everything is going to work out fine after all!"

"Carly, for heaven's sake! What are you talking about?"

"Grandma asked me what I wanted for my birthday and I said all I wanted was Captain. So Grandma took out an ad and this stable answered it and now Captain is going to Lincoln. Isn't it great!" Carly could hardly breathe, she was so excited.

Mom snatched the letter from Carly's hand and scanned it quickly. "I don't know what to say."

"Say 'Yes, Captain can go to Lincoln!' Can we call Grandma right now and tell her?"

"Carly, I can't say anything until Dad gets home and we've talked about it. You know that."

"But you're going to say yes, aren't you?"

"I don't know," Mom said, pursing her lips and frowning. "How will you get to the stables to work?"

"I don't know."

"Five miles is quite a long ways to ride a bike or walk every day, especially in the winter. Someone will most likely have to take you."

"You'd do that, wouldn't you, Mom? Please? For my sake, and Captain's?"

"Carly, don't beg," Mom said, but Carly could see the smile she was trying to hide. "I said we'd talk about it tonight, with Dad. Now, I have things to do, and so do you."

"Okay, Mom. Whatever you say, Mom. We'll talk with Dad tonight, Mom!" Carly took one giant step backward with each of her sentences. Mom laughed at her silliness and Carly knew, for the first time in a long time, that everything really was going to be all right!

Chapter 18
A Big Problem

The minute Dad walked in the door that night, Carly rushed to him and threw her arms around him.

"Wow!" he said. "What's this for?"

"Here!" Carly waved Grandma's letter in front of him. "Read this. The best news ever! Captain is going to Lincoln with me after all!"

"What?" Dad looked over at Mom and she nodded.

"It's true," Mom said. "My mom found a stable that will board Captain for free, as long as Carly agrees to work for them in the summertime and after school."

Dad took the letter out of Carly's hand and studied it. She held her breath. He wasn't going to say no, was he? Not when she was so close to getting what she wanted?

He threw the letter down on the table and picked Carly up. "Whoopee!" he shouted, as he twirled her around and around in a circle, like he used to do when she was a little girl. Carly squealed and her mom giggled. Then all three of them danced into the living room and collapsed on the sofa, laughing and talking at once.

"But how did this happen?" Dad asked.

"It was Grandma's gift to me," Carly said. "We didn't want to say anything to you, in case nobody answered her ad. We didn't want you to get your hopes up or anything."

"I knew you two were up to something," Mom said. "All that whispering behind my back!"

The ringing of the phone interrupted their celebration. "I'll bet that's Grandma, wondering if I got her letter," Carly said. "I can't wait to thank her!"

But it wasn't Grandma on the other end of the line. It was Luke.

"Carly, I did it! I did it!"

"Did what?"

"Convinced my mom and dad to buy Captain."

"But—" Carly tried to tell him about Grandma's letter. But Luke wouldn't stop talking.

"And it wasn't easy, believe you me! Dad liked the idea right off, just like you said he would. But not Mom. It took us all night to convince her. It wasn't until Josie got into the act that she finally said yes."

"But—" Carly tried again.

"Wait!" Luke said. "Josie's here. She wants to talk to you."

"No!" Carly shouted, but it was too late.

"Thank you, thank you, thank you!" Josie shouted on the line. "I never thought I would have my own horse. And now I have the bestest horse ever!"

"I—" Carly wasn't sure what to say. What could she say? How could she say the words that would break Josie's heart?

Then suddenly Luke was back on the phone again. "We've got to go, Carly. It's time to eat supper."

"Luke! Don't hang up. I need to tell you something!" But there was no answer. The line was dead.

"Carly, what was that all about?" Mom asked. She and Dad were standing by the sink, staring at her.

"Mom, Dad, I have a big problem. And I'm not sure how I'm going to fix it!"

Chapter 19

The Spoiledest Kid

Carly moaned and rolled over in bed, covering her head with her pillow. She had tossed and turned most of the night, trying to figure out a way to tell Josie that Captain wasn't for sale. But maybe she was worrying for nothing. Maybe Josie wouldn't be as upset as Carly thought. After all, the Carstens were sure to buy her another horse sometime. Once Carly explained it to Josie, she'd understand. Wouldn't she?

She tried to imagine Josie's face when she told her. And Carly realized that she couldn't do it. It would be too hard. She would have to call Luke on the phone and tell him, and he could tell Josie.

But was this the kind of news she could tell Luke over the telephone? Mr. Winters had shown up in person when he had backed out of the sale. Carly hadn't realized until now how much courage that had taken.

Thinking about Mr. Winters made her think about Savannah, as well. What would she do in this situation? Carly wasn't even sure why that thought was in her head. But now that it was there, she couldn't make it go away. Savannah would tell Josie she was keeping Captain and not think a thing about it, wouldn't she? Or would she?

Whose idea was it really, to back out of the sale? Dad said Mr. Winters was an honest man and a good judge of horses. Would he really have backed out of the sale just because of Captain's fall? Or had Savannah asked him to do it? Probably. She was probably scared to ride him.

Or maybe she was just trying to be nice. Maybe she was trying to do the right thing. Maybe you should think about that for a bit. Carly put her hands over her ears and closed her eyes, trying to drown out Grandpa's voice. But she couldn't. Then Grandpa's voice was joined by others. *Captain was meant to live in the country. It's time to stop fighting and accept what's happening. You're the spoiledest kid I know.*

"I'm not!" she said. "I'm not! Stop saying that!" Carly was shocked to hear her voice, angry and fearful. She looked around. There was no one else with her, except the voices in her head.

She sighed and threw the pillow on the floor. She knew what she had to do. She had known it last night, from the moment she'd hung up the phone. She just hadn't wanted to face it. She rolled out of bed and headed for the door. She needed to talk to Captain and she needed to do it, now.

Chapter 20
The Decision

Carly watched from the kitchen window as the Carsten's red pickup truck turned into the lane.

"They're here," Dad called from the back porch.

"I know. I'll be there in a minute." She took one last look at the photo in her hand. It was a picture of Josie and her, sitting double on Captain. Josie's grin was bigger than the whole rest of her face. Carly set the photo on the counter and headed for the door.

Dad waited outside. "Are you sure you want to do this?" he asked.

"I'm sure I don't want to do this," Carly said. "But it's what I'm going to do."

Dad put his arms around Carly's shoulders and gave her a hug. "Did I happen to tell you lately how proud

I am of you?" he asked.

Carly buried her face in Dad's shoulder for just a minute. "Thanks," she whispered. Then she looked up at him and forced a smile. "Let's get this over with."

Mr. Carsten was waiting for them at the corral. Josie jumped up and down beside him.

"Hi, Squirt," Carly said as she walked up to them. "Where's Luke? Didn't he come, too?"

"Nope," Josie said, as she threw her arms around Carly and hugged her. "Just me!"

"I had some things I needed him to do at home," Mr. Carsten added. He stuck his hand out and Dad grabbed it.

"Good to see you, Frank," Dad said. "Carly tells me you're interested in buying Captain for this girl of yours."

"That's right, I am. That is, assuming you still plan to sell him."

Dad looked over at Carly. This was her chance. All she had to do was tell Mr. Carsten about the letter and Captain would still be hers.

Carly looked down at Josie, who was staring up at her with a look of pure happiness on her face. "Yes, sir," Carly said. "Captain is still for sale. And like I told

Luke, I can't think of anyone I'd rather have buy him." Carly pushed the words past her lips and tried to tell herself she really meant them. She felt a knot forming in the back of her throat. She swallowed to force it down so she could breathe. Suddenly, she realized Mr. Carsten was talking again.

"I do have a favor to ask of you, Carly," he said.

"What's that?"

"I was wondering if, next summer, you could come back and spend a couple of weeks at our place, to get Josie started with Captain."

"You mean, you want me to give Josie riding lessons?" Carly asked, frowning.

"Not riding lessons, exactly," Mr. Carsten said. "After all, she's been riding Flash for years. So she knows the basics and all. But she hasn't had much experience with a horse like Captain."

"What about Luke?" Carly asked. "He could teach her just as much as I could."

"He could if he would. But you know how those two fight." Mr. Carsten reached down and tousled the hair on Josie's head before continuing. "Besides, my wife and I would rather have you do it. No one knows this horse better than you."

He looked at Carly and smiled. "What do you say? Are you interested? We'd pay you for your time."

"Pay me? Just to come back and spend time with Captain? Are you serious?" She looked up at her father. "What do you think, Dad? Can I do it?"

"It's up to you, Carly. But I think it's a great idea."

Carly looked at Captain. He stood patiently in the corral, watching them. Could she do it? Could she come back and help Josie with Captain, knowing that he wasn't her horse anymore? Knowing he never would be her horse again?

"What do you think?" she asked Josie. "Do you want me to teach you how to barrel race and pole bend?"

"Sure," Josie said, grinning. "You're the best. And if you teach me, then I'll be the best, too!"

Carly nodded her head in agreement. "That's right, Squirt," she said. "And don't you ever let your brother tell you otherwise!"

"So, do we have a deal?" Mr. Carsten asked.

"Yes, Sir, I guess we do," she said, shaking Mr. Carsten's hand. Then she pointed to Captain, who was watching over the corral fence. "Looks like Captain is ready for a ride," she said. "Josie, why don't we tell him the news, and get those lessons started right now!"

93446009R00078

Made in the USA
San Bernardino, CA
08 November 2018